NEW YORK TIMES BESTSELLING AUTHOR

EMMA HART

the accidental girlfriend

Copyright © by Emma Hart 2019

First Edition

All rights reserved. No part of this publication may be reproduced, distributed, or transmitted in any form or by any means, including photocopying, recording, or other electronic or mechanical methods, without the prior written permission of the publisher, except in the case of brief quotations embodied in critical reviews and certain other non-commercial uses permitted by copyright law.

Cover Design by Emma Hart
Editing by Ellie at My Brother's Editor
Formatting by Alyssa at Uplifting Designs & Marketing

the accidental girlfriend

CHAPTER ONE

Lauren

"I CAN'T REMEMBER a time I didn't have hemorrhoids."

I jerked my head up from my phone and looked at my sister. "I'm sorry, *what?*"

She sighed, adjusting her shirt so that she wasn't suffocating the six-week-old baby currently at her boob. "I miss pooping without worrying one of them is going to pop. I mean, is it not enough I pushed a human through my vagina? Now I have to live with little growths coming out of my anus?"

I blinked at her. "That is way more information than I ever needed to know about your anal region."

"Well, nobody else will listen to me."

"There's a reason for that, Isobel. It's because nobody cares about your hemorrhoids except your doctor." I put my phone screen-down on my knees. "Nobody forced you to procreate. It was entirely your own choice."

She sighed. "I blame Jared."

"Your husband can't take all the blame. You were the one who stopped your birth control."

"You're my little sister. Why aren't you on my side?"

"Because your side is ridiculous." I put my phone on the coffee table and headed for the door of my apartment when the doorbell rang. "I'm not going to sit here and eat pizza while you discuss the state of your asshole, so find something else to talk about!" I yelled back as I pulled the door open.

The poor pizza guy froze. He couldn't have been older than seventeen, and the red ballcap that was pulled over his forehead wasn't quite enough to hide both his horror and the spots that dotted his chin.

I looked down at the three boxes he had stacked on his hand and offered him a bright smile. "How much do I owe you?"

"I, uh, um…"

"I got it!" The voice of one of my best friends, Madi, echoed through the hall. "Is fifty enough?" she trilled, bouncing up behind him, her scarlet-colored curls flouncing around her shoulders.

"It's three pizzas. I should hope it does, or we're being ripped off," Tina grumbled, walking up behind her.

"Forty-one-ninety-eight," the pizza guy mumbled.

Madi waved two twenties and a ten at him. "Here you go, sweetie. Keep the change."

Someone got paid today.

"And there's my monthly girls' night paid for," she said happily, taking the boxes and dancing into my apartment. "What up, Iz? How's the asshole?"

I pinched the bridge of my nose and sighed.

Tina slipped her hand into her scarlet-red purse that matched her lips to a tee and pulled out a wallet. I hid a smile as she extracted ten dollars from it and handed it to the pizza guy, whispering, "For your mental trauma."

Mental trauma was about right.

I didn't see him delivering our pizza again anytime soon.

Or ever.

I didn't blame him. If I could get out of conversations about my sister's bodily parts, I would.

I'd lead the freakin' march.

I detoured into the kitchen to grab a bottle of wine and three glasses before joining everyone back in the living room. Madi had taken the seat next to my sister on the sofa and she'd tied her hair up into a messy topknot that matched her 'people hater' t-shirt and yoga pants perfectly.

Tina was on the armchair with her socked feet tucked beneath her butt, her dark hair hanging in a thick braid over one shoulder. That left me the oversized bean bag, but that was fine with me.

The bean bag was closer to the pizza.

I dropped onto the huge, fluffy seat with the glasses clinking in my hand.

"Uh, excuse me?" Isobel looked at the glasses as I set them down one-by-one on the coffee table. She'd put her boob away while I'd answered the door and Cara was sleeping in her crib.

Which I looked at before I replied to her. "You're breastfeeding."

"And? I can have a small glass of wine. Besides, these things are like a cattle farm." She cupped her boobs. "There's milk everywhere, including in your freezer."

I paused. "I'm not sure how I feel about having your breastmilk in my freezer."

"It's for when you babysit."

"I don't remember agreeing to that. Not that I don't love Cara, but I love sleep more."

She snorted as she leaned forward and unscrewed the wine, pouring a half-glass for herself. "Don't talk to me about sleep."

Madi looked between us. "I'll get another glass then, shall I?"

I nodded with a grim smile. If Iz wanted a glass of wine, she was going to have one. She'd been deprived for months—if you asked her, and as her younger sister, I never did.

"So," Tina said, leaning forward to lay out the pizza boxes. "What's new since last week?"

The rich scent of melted cheese filled the air, and Madi arrived with both paper plates and a wine glass with a flourish.

Excellent. No dishes.

I was winning at adulting this week.

Sure, my sister was keeping a tiny human alive, but I was minimizing my dishes one by one. Who was really nailing it?

"Well, my date last night sucked," Madi said, sliding a slice of ham and pineapple pizza onto her paper plate. "He totally catfished me. He was easily pushing fifty and did not have the body his Tinder profile said he did."

"I told you to ditch that app," I muttered around a mouthful of pepperoni and cheese. "It's the worst."

Tina nodded in solidarity. "I've never been happier since I deleted it from my phone."

"Yeah, well, I like it." Madi paused. "Most of the time."

"It's fifty-fifty," Iz said. "Jared's sister has been using it since her breakup. I helped her look through some guys and hoooooey, some are a treat, but the rest of them..."

"They should be euthanized," Tina finished. "They're either married, catfishing, or their looks are prettier than their personalities."

"I'll drink to that!" I raised my wine glass, and we all clinked. "All right, so Madi's date was a bust, Iz visited her doctor to complain about things she decided to put her body through—Tina?"

She chewed, looking up thoughtfully. "I think I'm going to adopt a cat."

"Really? You do know they're assholes, don't you?" As if he'd been called, my gray-and-white cat, Henry, strolled into the room. He studied us all with dark brown eyes before pausing by Cara's crib and sniffing it for a moment. Seemingly unimpressed, as was his default mood, he trotted over to us and looked at all of us.

Then he bounded up onto the sofa and plopped on top of Iz's head.

I bit the inside of my cheek. I swear I wasn't laughing. Okay, maybe I was a little bit. She was sitting there with a slice of pizza hanging out of her mouth and my cat on her head. She looked utterly ridiculous, especially when Henry flicked his tail around to stroke her cheek.

"Lauren," she said slowly. "Your cat is sitting on my head."

Honestly, there was no way to reply to that, was there? Except there should have been because Henry had issues.

Henry liked sitting on people's heads. He always had, ever since I'd brought him home from the shelter when he was nine months old. It'd been cute to start with, but now he, well. He wasn't exactly a small, cute kitten anymore. In fact, he probably needed to go on a diet.

It wasn't comfortable when a fat cat sat on your head.

With a sigh, I got up and walked over to her. Henry meowed his displeasure as I extracted him from my sister's head and deposited him in the hallway next to his scratching tower.

"We've talked about this," I said to him. "If you have to sit on people's heads, at least have enough manners to wait until they're done eating."

He mewled, turning around and showing me his butt.

Such a polite boy.

Rolling my eyes, I left him to sulk and probably pee in one of my shoes. "There. He'll leave us alone now."

"Until he wants one of our heads later," Madi pointed out. "Back to catching up. Recap: Iz went to the doctor, I got catfished, and Tina wants to adopt a cat who doesn't sit on people's heads. What's up with you, Lauren? Please have something juicy. The older we get, the less crazy these girls' nights are getting."

"The last time we went out, you were the one who got tired at nine-thirty and wanted to go to bed," I reminded her.

She groaned, reaching for her wine. "The shoes, man. They're so high, and there's only so many times I can be perved at by kids."

"Those kids are only four years younger than you, and it's easily solved by either wearing a fake engagement ring, pretending to be a lesbian, or simply wearing a shirt that covers your tits," Iz pointed out.

"She has a point," Tina said around a mouthful of food. "Just wear a sweater and sneakers. Problem solved."

"When did this become a shame Madi party?" She sniffed and leaned back with two slices of pizza on her plate. "And Lauren still hasn't told us what's new with her."

Three pairs of eyes turned to me, but only my sister was smirking.

Because she knew.

Nothing.

There was a big fat nothing new with me.

"Um…" I grabbed another slice of pizza before setting my plate on the floor in front of me. "I looked for new curtains for my bedroom?"

"Lauren," Tina groaned. "How is that exciting?"

"How is thinking about adopting a cat exciting? I've done it. Look at where it got me."

Iz pulled a hair from her mouth. "She's not wrong."

Madi leaned forward, pushing a loose curl behind her ear. "Curtains, Grandma? Really? You work in a bar. Are you telling me that nobody asked for your number? Did nobody eye you up? Nobody wanted to bend you over and—"

Cara cut her off with a snuffle.

We all froze. I don't think any of us breathed for a good ninety seconds until my niece filled the room with sucking sounds as she made good work of her pacifier.

"Do you dirty?" Madi finished on a whisper.

I stared flatly at her and drained my wine. "The only person who hit on me this week was Mr. Hennington, and that's because he's trying to get a free beer out of me."

"Did it work?" Iz asked brightly.

"No! He's eighty-five!"

"And proof that drinking every day is good for you. Cheers!" Tina raised her glass and quickly finished it.

I topped off both our glasses and headed to the kitchen for the second bottle. "Look," I said as I resumed my position on the beanbag, uncapping the bottle to finish pouring my glass. "Kelsey left last week, and I'm picking up her shifts. The only hot dates I'm getting are with Kenny the delivery driver, and he's as attractive as a pig in shit."

"Hey, some people like pigs," Iz said. With pizza sauce smeared all over her chin. Presumably proving her own point.

Madi passed her a napkin and tapped her own jaw.

"Besides, I don't need to date. I'm happy with my life as it is," I continued, leaning back in the beanbag. "I don't have time to date. It's bad enough with a cat needing my attention, never mind a man wanting me to love him."

Tina lifted her glass. "I hear that."

"Speak for yourselves," Iz added. "I have two humans who need me. I'd love to be single."

Madi side-eyed her as she poured her second glass. "No, you wouldn't. If you were single, you'd have to run to the store and buy your own Twinkies."

Iz sighed. "Do you know how long it takes me to get out the door these days? Going to Target requires packing for a mini vacay twice over, and I'm still going to forget something."

"Ah," I said. "But you decided to birth a crotch goblin. You don't get to complain about needing a suitcase to spend two hundred dollars when you meant to spend twenty."

"Okay, literally everyone gets to complain about that," Tina said, dangling her glass between her fingers. "Target is a cesspit of temptation."

"Like Tinder!" Madi snapped her fingers. "A cesspit of temptation and lies."

I blinked at my best friends. That had escalated rather quickly. I mean, she wasn't wrong.

Tinder told me the hot twenty-eight-year-old had muscles on his muscles and a great job, but he was actually fifty-two with a beer belly and was a trash guy.

Target told me I only needed Post-It notes and Cheetos, but I left with Post-It notes, Cheetos, socks, three tank tops, two bags of Hershey's kisses, hand soap, dishcloths, and toilet cleaner. Plus a twenty-eight pack of toilet tissue and eighty-nine sanitary towels.

Iz snapped her fingers. "I know. We should get Lauren a date."

"Yes!" Madi punched the air. "Let's get Lauren a date!"

"Let's not," I said quickly. "Lauren's fine. Lauren doesn't need a date. Lauren has a vibrator."

Tina grinned. "When you use a vibrator as an excuse, you need a date."

"On the contrary," I replied. "A vibrator is the perfect excuse *not* to date. It doesn't argue with me. It doesn't expect anything from me. It doesn't have dirty clothes. It doesn't talk to me during my favorite TV shows. And, when I'm done with it, I can put it in a drawer until I need it again. Do you know what happens if you stuff a man in a drawer? You get put in prison. So until a time that the vibrators rise up and start marching for rights for sex toys while wearing slogan t-shirts, I'm all good."

"Why would vibrators start marching for sex toy rights?" Madi asked. "They don't have legs. They can't march."

"Turn them on and they can move." Tina nodded. "They can buzz along."

"Still preferable to men," Iz said. "They won't argue, even when they're marching. Not to mention that it'd take them a while to get to where they needed to go. Men? Nope. They come like Usain Bolt looking at a world record."

This was going downhill. Fast.

"Look, the point is, nobody needs to stage a protest for sex toys to have rights." I raised my hands. "I'm good with Jerry. Jerry's good with me. We're both satisfied. I do not need any of you guys to find me a date."

CHAPTER TWO

Lauren

YOU KNOW HOW people say, 'famous last words?'

Yeah. I was now the lucky duck on the receiving end of what, exactly, that phrase meant.

Apparently, nobody cared if I wanted a date or not. The wine had put a hive of bees in their bonnets, and now, my two best friends and my too-sober-for-this-shit sister were trawling dating websites.

It was the stupidest thing I'd ever been privy to. They'd been through at least twenty-five profiles and discarded every single one of them. It was a waste of time because I didn't even need to look at the profiles to tell them that they were all not my type.

Not even close.

"I know." Tina waved the full bottle of wine. The third bottle. "None of these are working! I have an idea!"

Oh, God.

"Why don't we bring the hot guys to Lauren?"

"Like a farm show? Or an auction?" Iz asked, ignoring Madi's snort-laughing. "Are we going to put Lauren on a pedestal and line guys up in front of her?"

"We could send her on *The Bachelor* or *The Bachelorette*," Madi offered. "*The Bachelorette* is probably better. The guys really will come to her, and have you seen the men they rustle up for that thing? It's like a supermarket full of snacks over there."

I had no idea what that meant.

"No, no reality shows," I said quickly. "You guys, really, I'm good. I'm fine. You don't need to—"

I was interrupted by a gasp from Tina. She filled up all four empty wine glasses on the table, giving Iz her second, tiny glass. Literally. It was all of two mouthfuls. I guess she wanted her to be included in whatever cockamamie plan she'd thought up now.

"We put out an ad online!"

"No." I vehemently shook my head. "No. Absolutely not."

"Like on Craigslist?" Madi sat upright. "That's not a bad idea."

"It's a terrible idea!"

Iz leaned forward. "Actually, that's not so bad. The chance of catfishing would be seriously reduced. Statistically, there's a better chance of you actually meeting someone online outside of a dating website. There are no computer algorithms getting in the way and bumping page views. It'll be actual people seeing your ad."

What? How had this gone from getting me a date to pimping me out online?

This was escalating quickly. I wasn't a fan of this. I wasn't the only single one here. Why was I on the end of this?

I wanted to stamp my feet and scream into a pillow. This had not been my plan for girls' night—I'd wanted pizza, wine, and trashy TV. What the hell had been put in the wine to give these hooligans such ideas?

"This is a terrible idea," I said, scooting forward on the beanbag. "You cannot put an ad on a website like Craigslist and expect that I get a date."

"No, wait." Madi put one finger up. "A girl I work with sister's did it. She put up an ad saying that she wanted to be someone's date for the weekend because she was bored. She dated the guy for like eighteen months before they broke up because his work relocated him to Canada."

This was... Wow. This really was escalating.

I wasn't going to lie; this was getting uncomfortable. Severely so.

I took two big mouthfuls of wine. Why hadn't I put this to a stop straight away? They were getting carried away. I couldn't believe that they'd been talking about getting me a date for the last hour.

We'd eaten two and a half pizzas between us, and we were on wine bottle number three. Even Cara was awake and snorting to herself in her crib, sucking passionately on her pacifier. That was how riveting this conversation was.

A six-week-old baby had woken up for it.

Thankfully for me, it looked like she was on my side because the sound of the world's biggest wet fart came from her direction.

We all froze as a rancid smell came our way.

Iz sighed, getting up. "I'll take her upstairs and change her. Jesus, that's like a sack of dead fish," she muttered to herself as she grabbed the change bag and the baby.

Was this it? Had Cara done her aunt a solid and freed me from this Craigslist dating nonsense?

"Are we doing this, then?" Madi asked Tina as soon as Iz had left. "Let's put her online looking for a date!"

Well, that was a big fat no.

"A fake date." I was going to get my input before they got carried away. "If you're going to pimp me out to the internet, you can make it a fake date."

Tina paused. "Like an escort?"

"Not like an escort," I quickly corrected. "I'm not going to be paid. Jesus, what the hell do you think of me?"

Madi snorted wine up her nose. "Okay, no payment. So how do we word this, and where do we post it? Facebook? Instagram? Twitter? Craigslist?"

"What is your obsession with Craigslist?"

"You can get some good stuff on Craigslist. Don't diss it 'til you've tried it."

"Great. So now I'm just good stuff?"

"All four," Tina said brightly, putting an end to our bickering. "Why not? It'll maximize our chances of getting Lauren the virgin over here a date."

"A fake date!" I ran my fingers through my hair. "Oh, my God. Okay, fine. We'll do it, but when I'm done with this shit, we're doing the same for you two."

"As long as I get laid, I'm good." Madi held up her hands.

Tina wrinkled her face up. "Fine. Fair is fair."

I pulled my laptop from under the coffee table and hauled myself over to the sofa, taking the middle cushion. Tina took the chair to my left while Madi readjusted herself on the right side of me.

This was a terrible idea. It was going to be a horrible mistake. I didn't have to be a genius or a fortune teller to know that. All I could do at this point was ride the wave my drunken best friends had conjured up and go with it.

If I agreed, I had some form of control over this horrid idea.

Oh, God, what was I doing?

I signed into my computer and opened up a new document in Notepad. I wished I could take a moment to savor the taste of my wine, but I couldn't because it tasted like sadness and regret.

"You need your name, age, job, and a little about yourself." Tina shuffled in closer to me. "Start with your name!"

"No, really? I thought she should start with her cup size," Madi drawled.

"All right, all right, I got this. This is only a draft, anyway."

Yep. Regret was not a strong enough word for this…

Name: Lauren Green

Age: 25

Profession: I'd have to kill you if I told you

"Cute," Madi said. "Keep some suspense."

"How is bartending remotely suspenseful?" I asked her. "The biggest question I get asked is how much a fishbowl costs."

Tina rested her head on my shoulder. "Well, they won't know that you can drink them under the table. That's a nice surprise."

Yeah. It hadn't been a nice surprise for my cousins at my grandparents' fiftieth wedding anniversary. The sailor and the cop had been drunk under the table by little old me.

I was simultaneously proud and ashamed.

"Okay, about you. What can we say about you that doesn't tip them off to the fact you're a raging bitch for five days each month?" Madi slapped her lips together.

"A photo of a man," Iz said dryly, perching on the arm of the chair with Cara gurgling on her chest. "She's a woman. It's a given."

I glared at my sister. "Ugh. I don't know. I'll put something quirky." I hit the Enter key twice.

Offering my services as a fake date for one night only. Got a wedding you need a date for? I'm a classy girl in public with a dirty side in private. How about a family get-together where you're the only single grandchild going? This blue-eyed brunette with a passion for pizza is the one you've been looking for. Or if you're heading to a party and need to make that one person jealous—I've got an ass you could crack a diamond on.

Contact me at lauren.a.green@gmail.com or 857-6612-098 with your needs.

And no, I'm not charging.

But I'm not buying my own drinks either.

"There," I said, pushing the laptop over my thighs to my knees. "How's that?"

"Can't see," Iz said, positioning Cara on her shoulder to burp her.

"You might wanna move," I muttered to Tina as both Madi and I moved up.

Tina eyed the baby speculatively and used one of my cushions as a barrier between them. Madi read the ad copy out loud, stopping to snort at the mention of my ass cutting diamond.

It couldn't. The only thing my ass could cut was my dreams of fitting into a size eight pair of jeans.

A size ten, too, depending on whether or not Mother Nature was making her monthly visit.

A girl could put on the pounds when *that* bitch stopped by.

"Perfect," Iz said with a nod. "At the very least, anyone who responds to that will have a similar sense of humor to you."

"A warped one," Tina piped up.

"Hey, that's funny!" I pointed at the screen. "I'd date me."

Madi nudged me. "That's the point they're making. For what it's worth, I think it's fucking hilarious, too."

I rolled my eyes. "I guess I'll post it."

"No, you don't guess. You will." Tina took the laptop from me, nestling it on her own legs, and opened the internet browser.

I took the cushion she'd been using to separate her and Cara's spit and pressed my face into it. It was, thankfully, baby spit-free. Unlike my sister's shoulder that had a tasty trail of white-yellow goo over it.

Unbothered, Iz put Cara back down in the crib and used her foot to rock it back and forth. Madi eyed her for a moment, but Iz shut her down by saying, "Don't judge me. She's gonna wake me every two hours for boob juice."

That was the end of that as everyone turned their attention to the screen. Tina's fingers flew across the keyboard like little lightning bolts as she typed in what I'd written. At least, I hoped that was what she was typing.

Copy and pasting didn't require that many keys.

"Done!" She hit the left mouse button with a flourish and turned the screen toward me. She'd corrected a couple of typos I'd made and added in a couple of extra words, but it was otherwise exactly the same as the one I'd written up.

"Post it. Go ahead." I shook my head and leaned back on the sofa.

Right in time for Henry to bound up onto the back of the cushions, pad his way along, and sit his fat ass on my head.

That about summed it up.

♥

From: Kirsty Jackson (kjackson_305@hotmail.com)

To: Lauren Green (lauren.a.green@gmail.com)

Subject: Fake Date Ad

Hi Lauren,

I saw your ad on Craigslist early this morning when I was browsing. My brother is looking for a date for his ten-year high school reunion this Friday night. Are you free then?

Best,

Kirsty

I blinked at the email.

Holy shit, this was for real.

Henry meowed his displeasure as I sat up in bed, dislodging him from his sleeping place in the crook of my knees.

Someone had actually emailed me about that stupid ad that I'd been talked into placing last night. Why hadn't I thought that it would happen? I hadn't actually taken it seriously, but now, here I was...

Staring at an email from someone who was apparently emailing me on behalf of her brother.

I had no idea how I felt about this.

So, I did what any slightly-hungover, tired, and hungry woman would do. I opened up my three-way chat with Tina and Madi and sent them a screenshot.

```
TINA: OMG!!!! Are you doing it?
MADI: *ten laughing emojis*
LAUREN: This is no joke. What the
hell do I say????
MADI: Yes.
TINA: Yes.
```

I groaned. How did I know they were going to say that? I picked up my phone and slid out of bed, typing my response as I headed for the bathroom.

> LAUREN: I don't even know if I can. I think I'm working Friday's shift. Stella has a date.
>
> MADI: I saw her yesterday in the store and she was on the phone complaining about guys. Text her and see if she'll swap.

I really didn't want to text Stella. I liked her, but she was the kind of person who was larger than life. She had the brightest, bubbliest personality and she could talk the ears off of Dumbo. Working with her was hell because, while she was a hard worker, she tended to get wrapped up easily in conversations. Luckily, our boss knew that, so it wasn't often we worked together.

I didn't have a choice, though. If she would swap her Saturday shift for my Friday one—

Jesus, what the hell was I thinking? I wasn't really going to do this, was I?

Judging by the way my fingers pulled up the messaging app on my phone before I'd even gotten my ass off the toilet, apparently, I was.

> LAUREN: Hey, Stella. Do you still have that date on Friday?

I was mid-way through brushing my teeth and thankfully no longer on the toilet when my phone lit up with her reply.

> STELLA: Hey. No, I don't. It fell through. Why?

LAUREN: I might have one Friday and was wondering if we could swap our shifts this weekend. I have Friday 6-close.

STELLA: I have the same Saturday. I've got no plans. I don't mind swapping. Did you ask Pete?

LAUREN: No, I wanted to ask you first. I'll text him now.

I did just that before I headed downstairs. I was halfway through a bowl of cereal when Pete's name flashed on my screen with a message saying that he was fine with us swapping as long as I changed it on the schedule when I went into work.

That was it, then. I was actually doing this.

I needed to see a psychiatrist.

CHAPTER THREE
Mason

RUBBING ONE HAND through my hair, I covered my mouth with my hand to hide my yawn. The banging at my door was fucking relentless, and that meant there was only one person on the other side of it:

My little sister.

I paused to look through the peephole. Yep, sure as fucking shit, Kirsty was standing there, looking fresher than a field full of daisies.

Morning people like her needed to be shot.

I turned the key in the lock and undid the deadbolt before I tugged it open a crack. "What?"

She grinned, her dark brown eyes sparkling. "I have a surprise for you."

"No." I pushed the door shut and turned around.

"Mason!" She banged on the door again. "I'm going to

stand here and bang until you let me in!"

I groaned and stopped mid-step. If it were anyone else, I'd leave them there looking like an idiot. The problem was, I knew my sister, and I knew she wasn't damn well lying. She'd set up camp outside if she had to.

Not to mention that my neighbor, Mrs. Allerton, was the nosiest woman on this planet. She loved nothing more than looking through her peephole at the comings and goings of everyone in the building, and since I lived opposite her, I was her primary target.

She also hated noise, being interrupted during her TV shows, and just about everything else.

"Fine. Just stop banging," I called, going back to the door. I yanked it open at the same time the door on the other side of the hall did.

Oh, fuck it.

Mrs. Allerton hobbled out, her stick tapping extra loudly against the floor. Her beady dark eyes were hidden behind huge spectacles that took up half of her wrinkled face, and her white hair was still styled in rollers.

She clutched her robe tighter to her chest. "Mason? Mason, is that you making that racket?"

Kirsty swallowed. "Sorry, Mrs. Allerton. That was me knocking on his door."

"Knocking on his door?" She leaned in to see her. "Oh, Kirsty. Couldn't you call? I thought it was a bombing."

Sweet Jesus...

"I'm sorry. I didn't mean to disturb you."

"No, no, it's fine. You young people have no respect for the news anymore. I only wanted to see what was going on in the world, but here I was, thinking I'd be on the news tomorrow."

She'd started it now.

"Do you know there's a fellow at the water plant who got poisoned with syphilis?"

"I did not," Kirsty said politely.

"Mmm. I'll have to see how he got poisoned. See if I can do that for noisy neighbors." She adjusted her glasses and looked at us both. "Keep it down. Reruns of *Wheel of Fortune* are about to come on, and I don't like to be interrupted during them."

I held up my hands. "No more noise, Mrs. Allerton, I promise. I apologize for my sister's rudeness."

"See that you're right." She grunted and, after a painfully slow turn, shuffled back into her apartment, her stick still thumping against the ground.

"I'd hate to live beneath her," Kirsty muttered, shoving past me into my apartment.

"Mmph." She had a point; the woman liked to complain about noise, yet she was the noisiest one of everyone in the building. "What do you want, Kirst?"

"I have a surprise for you," she repeated, this time a lot brighter. "You're going to love it."

"I doubt that." I scratched my balls and walked into the kitchen ahead of her.

"Do you have to do that?"

"Do what?"

"Scratch your balls when I'm around."

"Yep." I reached down and did it again for good measure. "You banged on my door and you woke me up. You can handle me having an itch, Kirsty."

She wrinkled her face up in disgust. "You're gross."

"Yep. What do you want?"

She put her purse on the kitchen island and hopped onto one of the stools. "I have some good news for you."

"I doubt it." I switched the coffee machine on.

"No, it is, I swear."

"Again, I doubt it, but I'll humor you." Turning, I leaned against the counter and folded my arms across my chest. "What's the so-called good news?"

She leaned forward and grinned. "I got you a date for Friday night."

She did what?

I blinked at her. Was I hearing her right? Was she seriously telling me that she had me a date for Friday night? For the high school reunion I was only attending because my also-single best friend was making me?

Fuck me dead. My sister had lost it.

"You did what?" I finally managed to say.

"I got you a date," she said, seemingly unbothered by the fact I was not happy.

Actually, she probably knew, she was just fucking ignoring me. The little shit.

"Kirsty, I don't want a date," I said slowly. "I planned on going in, showing my face, and getting the fuck out of that hellhole."

She shook her head. "You need a date."

"I beg to differ." I hit the button on the coffee machine.

It spat steam before it released the milk that came out before the coffee. "I don't need a date. I don't need anything. I'm going with Trev."

"You can't go to your reunion with your best friend. You're not a woman."

"I also can't go on a first date there with a woman."

"Ah, see, this is the best part! It's not a real date."

She was going to give me whiplash by the time she left.

"What are you talking about? Did you drink an espresso again? You know those make you hyper." I pulled my cup from beneath the machine and added two sugars.

Kirsty groaned. "Listen—I was on Craigslist—"

"No good story ever started with that."

"And I was browsing, as you do, and I found this ad that made me laugh. Hold on, let me get it and I'll read it for you."

"You're good, Kirst, really. I'm not taking a date."

"No, no, you are. She has the same weird sense of humor as you do. You just have to pretend to like her."

"No pressure, then."

"Listen to this! She's a hoot!" She sat up a little straighter. "Okay. Name: Lauren Green. Age: Twenty-five. Profession: I'd have to kill you if I told you.

"*Offering my services as a fake date for one night only. Got a wedding you need a date for? I'm a classy girl in public with a dirty side in private. How about a family get-together where you're the only single grandchild going? This blue-eyed brunette with a passion for pizza is the one you've been looking for. Or if you're heading to a party and need to make that one person jealous—I've got an ass you could crack a diamond on. Contact me at lauren.a.green@ gmail.com or 857-6612-098 with your needs. And no, I'm not charging. But I'm not buying my own drinks either."*

Against my will, I snorted.

All right, I would admit it. Once.

Whoever this Lauren was, she was good.

"Kirsty, no." I shook my head. "I'm not taking a date, much less a stranger."

She bit her lower lip. "Problem."

"If you tell me you already emailed her and set it up—"

"Okay, then, I won't."

I put my coffee cup down and buried my face in my hands. She had to be joking. There was no way she'd emailed a total stranger based upon a humorous Craigslist ad and set me up with the writer of said ad.

Was there?

Wait, scratch that shit.

This was my sister. My annoying younger sister who'd made it her life's mission to get all up in my business at every available opportunity.

She had.

She'd emailed this Lauren girl.

"Kirsty..." I pinched the bridge of my nose and peered over at her. "Don't tell me you've emailed her and set this up."

She held her hands up and scooted the stool back a little. "Like I said, I won't."

"For fuck's sake!"

"She's gonna be there!" Kirsty stood up and pointed at me. "Do you want to show up there, single, while she's flaunting her piece of shit?"

My jaw tightened as I gritted my teeth. "Claudia's business is no longer mine. I couldn't give a fuck if she shows up in a horse-drawn carriage with some foreign prince on her arm. She cheated. I ended it. It is what it is."

"She's going to take him, and you know it." She raised her eyebrows. "Do you really want to show up with freaking Trevor of all people?"

"I don't give a shit what Claudia does. She can go with who she pleases. I'm not going to go with some strange woman to make a point to a woman I no longer care about."

"Come on. It's been five months. Just long enough for you to move on but not so much that you don't care about what she's doing."

"I don't care." I passed her a cup of coffee. "Honestly, Kirst, I don't. I haven't thought about her in weeks. I don't need to take some stranger to an event I couldn't give a shit about just to get under her skin."

Kirsty stirred some sugar into her coffee. "Sure you do. It'll be funny."

I side-eyed her as she sipped. "I'm glad my life is a source of amusement for you. I'm not taking anyone to the reunion."

"Oh, come on. You know what Claudia's like. She's going to lord her new relationship over you."

"I could show up with Naomi Campbell on my arm and she'd still lord it over me," I replied dryly. "I'm not taking a stranger."

"Then meet her before. She won't be a stranger then."

"You've lost your damn mind."

"Can't lose something I never had." She grinned. "Besides, she's already swapped her shift to go."

I pinched the bridge of my nose again. I didn't need to get my eyes tested to see that I was fighting a losing battle. She'd organized this fully behind my back because she knew I wouldn't agree to it.

She was a pain in my fucking ass.

"Just do it," Kirsty said. "I'll give you her number so you can text before. At least you'll know a little about each other. And, if you're really only staying an hour, then it won't be hard to fake it."

I sighed and leaned forward in despair. "Fine. Give me her number."

And I'd use it to cancel the damn date.

♥

MASON: Hi. This is Mason. My sister Kirsty gave me your number.

I had no idea what else to say to her to open this line of conversation. It was the most awkward fucking thing I'd ever done, and I'd once ended up on a blind date with a woman old enough to be my mother.

Still didn't know how that'd happened.

Oh, that's right—the internet happened.

I swigged from my beer and ran my fingers through my still-wet hair. Lauren's number had been burning a hole in my pocket all day when I was at work to the point that I'd been distracted and almost plastered my own thumb to a wall.

I glanced at my phone. Still no reply. Why would there be? It'd been fucking minutes.

Jesus Christ, this was going to be the end of me.

It was why I had to cancel it. My nosy ass sister was a thorn in my side, and this date was not a good thing.

I'd meant it when I'd told her that I couldn't give a flying, dancing shit about my ex-fiancé. Claudia Simmons was nobody to me now. That'd changed the moment I'd found her in bed with one of her boss six months ago.

She'd thrown six years of a relationship down the drain for a quick roll in the hay.

She could stay there. She was nothing more than a social climber, and while I'd been thinking about spending my life with her, she'd been thinking about how she could level up and find someone richer than me.

It bugged her more than anything that I was happy to be a builder. That I was content in my "little person's job," as she'd once called it.

It was no wonder that I wasn't all for dating, really.

My phone buzzed with an incoming text message. Lauren's name appeared on the screen, and I picked it up to see her response.

> LAUREN: Hi. I'm Lauren. Your sister said you'd text.

Jesus, was Kirsty striking up a friendship with this—admittedly witty—stranger?

> MASON: Look, I need to be honest. She set this up entirely. I wasn't looking for a date for the reunion.

Her response was swift.

> LAUREN: Ah. I did wonder. So you don't need a date?
>
> MASON: She responded to your ad because my ex is going to be at the reunion. She hates her and thinks I should have revenge by taking someone with me. I'm sorry she wasted your time.
>
> LAUREN: Don't worry about it. Honestly, I only put up the stupid ad because my friends and sister were on my back about dating. I didn't think anyone would actually respond to it, so the joke was on me.

I cracked a smile at that. If I was honest, it was the exact kind of ad I would have responded to if I'd actually needed a date.

> MASON: For what it's worth, I'd have responded if I needed one. It was pretty fucking funny.
>
> LAUREN: Thanks. I was going for off-putting and unattractive, but pretty fucking funny works.
>
> MASON: You probably shouldn't have put the part about being dirty between the sheets. That's not how to write an unattractive ad.
>
> LAUREN: Yeah, in hindsight, that was the wine talking.

MASON: It didn't help your cause.

LAUREN: I know that now.

LAUREN: Can I be nosy?

MASON: My sister wasted your time, so I suppose I can't say no.

LAUREN: LOL. That's the most begrudging agreement I've ever gotten.

LAUREN: Okay. What did your ex do that was so bad that your sister tried to set you up with a fake date just to get at her?

I should have known that was coming.

MASON: She cheated on me after six years with her boss. It was around six months ago.

LAUREN: Whoa, shit, I'm sorry.

MASON: Don't worry. I'm over it—Kirsty apparently isn't.

LAUREN: I guess your ex is going to be at the reunion?

ME: Yeah. We got together when she came home after college. Kirsty hates her, but I couldn't care less. I'm not looking forward to seeing her, but it's not the end of the world.

LAUREN: I'm sorry.

MASON: It's ok. Really. I guess Kirsty thought me taking a date would get under her skin.

LAUREN: Would it?

MASON: Maybe. She's that kind of person. If she can't have it, nobody can.

LAUREN: Wow. You're a good person. I'd be finding the hottest person imaginable and climbing them like a koala in a eucalyptus tree in front of my ex if I were you. I'd rub it in their face so hard they'd get a free facial.

I laughed. Shit, she was a hoot. And was she right? Was I a good person for not wanting to rub anything in Claudia's face after what she did to me?

LAUREN: Look, I'm just throwing it out there: I changed my shift anyway and I don't have any plans. If you decide that you want to be petty, I don't mind being your fake girlfriend. I'll even climb you like a tree if you want me to.

Fuck it. I had nothing to lose. If nothing else, she sounded like she'd be a really good time.

MASON: All right, you twisted my arm. They rented out the function room at The Beachside. Send me your address, and I'll pick you up at six-forty-five.

CHAPTER FOUR

Lauren

*I*N HINDSIGHT, THIS had all been a terrible idea, from beginning to end.

What in the ever-loving fuck was I doing? I knew nothing about Mason Jackson except what I'd learned from our brief text conversations, and even that had been the basics so that I didn't look like a total fool when I pretended to be his girlfriend.

He was twenty-eight and worked as a builder. His grandpa had recently moved in with his parents, Mason's favorite movie was *The Equalizer*, and his favorite food was buffalo chicken wings.

That was all I needed to know to get through the night.

In return, I'd told him that I was twenty-five, worked as a bartender, lived alone, and had a new baby niece. My favorite movie was *Mean Girls* and my favorite food was cheeseburgers.

That was all *he* needed to get through the night.

I was a little more comfortable knowing that the reunion was at the bar where I worked. It meant I wasn't totally alone, because Stella would probably be working the bar in the function room.

It was weird to think that, if I'd kept the shift, I likely would have met Mason anyway.

I shuddered that thought off and looked at myself in the mirror. My strapless, bright-pink dress seemed a little overkill, but it was my date dress. Not that it was a lucky charm or anything, because if it was, I wouldn't be single and wouldn't need a date dress, but it was The Dress.

You know the one. Every woman has The Dress that flatters every part of their body. For me, it was this one. It hugged my boobs like a glove and was fitted to the waist where it flared out all flirty and girly.

It also hid the fluff on my hips, and any dress that could hide the extra few pounds was a dress you cherished.

At least if you were me. I was pretty sure the cheeseburgers went straight to my hips.

I slipped my feet into nude heels, then checked to make sure that my light-pink lipstick hadn't smudged.

Thankfully, it hadn't. I took a few seconds to run the brush through my straight, dark hair one more time, then tucked my lipstick into my clutch purse and headed to the living room.

A check of the time on my phone said Mason was running a few minutes late, and I headed to the kitchen to take a quick swig of wine for courage.

I felt…weird.

I didn't know how to describe it. This date put a whole new meaning on the idea of a first date, mostly because I had to pretend that I knew the guy whose face I'd never seen.

At some point during the past five days, we'd been casually texting each other, neither one of us had ever thought to ask the other for a picture.

Now, I was regretting it.

Jesus, what if he was ugly? Not that there was anything wrong with it, but I was going to my place of work with him. If he wasn't attractive, there'd be no getting away from what a disaster it would be.

That was shallow of me. I knew that. I wasn't exactly proud of it, but I wasn't going to lie and say that looks didn't matter to me.

Looks mattered to everyone.

We were biologically inclined to fall in love with and marry and procreate with the person we were most attracted to, and that started with looks.

Again: shallow.

But tell that to biology and evolution, not me. I was just a product of it all.

I was also not a great actress. Seriously. I only participated in one school play, and it'd been a complete disaster. I was not cut out for acting, which brought forth another question about why the hell I was doing this.

I literally had to act the entire night.

Act like I knew Mason.

Act like I was falling for him.

Act like I was attracted to him.

Him being hot was literally the only thing I had to grab onto right now. I needed him to be good looking so that I didn't have to fake hanging off him or, as I'd said to him in our very first conversation, climbing him like a tree.

Not that I'd do it in public. I wasn't actually a koala, but hey, it'd made him laugh.

Four knocks at my door made me freeze.

Oh, my God.

He was here.

Swallowing, I smoothed out my dress and approached the door. My hand shook as I reached for the handle and opened the door.

And laid eyes on the most beautiful fucking human being I'd ever seen in my life.

He was a few inches taller than me, even when I was in heels. Muscles filled out the white shirt that was undone at his neck and had the sleeves rolled up to his elbows. Light-wash jeans with a rip on each knee hugged his lower body, leading to shiny shoes that peeked out from beneath the bottom of the pants.

He had the thickest dark hair that was swept over to one side; long on top, short on the sides. Dark stubble decorated his chin and jaw, breaking only to reveal full, soft-looking lips that were currently curved up into a small smile.

And the eyes.

Motherfucker, those eyes.

Bright blue. Magnetic. All-consuming.

And they were focused on me, taking me in, from head to toe.

Holy shit, there was a God. And he'd heard my freakin' prayers because Mason Jackson was surely heaven-sent.

There would be zero problems pretending to climb this man like a tree.

I swallowed. Hard.

"Lauren?" he asked, a twinkle in his eye.

"That's me. Mason?" I replied, holding out my hand.

He looked at it with a flash of amusement before he took it, gripping it tightly. "That's me. Sorry I'm late—I got stuck in some traffic in town. Are you ready to go?"

"Yep. Let me grab my purse." I turned away from him, my eyes widening for a second.

Jesus, he was tall, he was hot, and he shook my hand in a way that said he could grip just about any part of my body and I'd freakin' love it.

I gripped my clutch and tucked it against my body. Thanks to early summer in Northern Florida, I didn't need a jacket, so I stepped out into the hall, making sure to lock my door behind me.

"Are you sure you're okay with this?" Mason asked, glancing at me as we waited for the elevator to reach my floor.

I nodded. "I advertised a fake date. Honestly, I'm fine with it. Besides—if it goes really bad, I work at The Beachside, so I can run away and hide from you."

He laughed. It was a delicious sound. Like melted ice cream on top of a hot chocolate brownie. That's what it would taste like if laughs could be eaten.

Hnnnnng.

Okay. I needed to get ahold of myself. This was going

to be a disaster if I didn't calm the fuck down.

I took a deep breath as I stepped into the elevator.

"You didn't mention that you work there," Mason said, hitting the button for the ground floor. "I've never been there."

"Really? I thought everyone in town had been to The Beachside."

"Nah. I'm more of a sports bar guy instead of a beach bar."

"It's not really a beach bar." I paused. "All right, kinda, but only because it's right on the beach."

"That makes it a beach bar." He chuckled. "Plus, they don't play sports or serve wings, and that's a deal breaker for me."

"Right. Your love affair with buffalo wings." I looked at him and tapped my temple. "See? I remembered."

He laughed as the elevator shuddered to the ground floor. Holding out his hand, he made sure the doors stayed open and motioned for me to exit first. "Honestly, if they served wings, I might go."

"Really? You can't eat anything but wings? They do great food. You'll see tonight. The party spreads are epic."

"Will there be wings?"

"No, but there won't be cheeseburgers either, and you don't see me complaining about it."

"I'm going to find your manager and tell him to serve wings. What kind of a bar doesn't serve wings?"

I pushed open the door to the building. "The kind who doesn't want sports yobs shouting at TVs?"

"Point well made." Mason shook his head. "I can't believe there are no wings."

"Okay, if you're gonna complain about it all night, I'm gonna have no problem pretending to be your girlfriend. I'll be rolling my eyes like it's my job."

He caught the door as he followed me out and smirked. "Well, that's how we're gonna do this. I'll complain, you roll your eyes, and everyone will believe this is a real relationship."

I rolled my eyes.

"That. Do that all night." He grinned and led me to his car, where he hit the button on his key fob and opened the passenger-side door for me. "That'll sell it."

I didn't want to roll my eyes again, but… I was going to have one hell of a headache by the end of the night at this rate.

"Maybe we can try something a little less headache-inducing," I said as he joined me from the driver side. "What kind of girlfriend would you like me to be? A simpering thing who hangs off your arm and laughs at everything? An independent woman who can do everything but buy her own drinks? I'll warn you now; I'm a terrible actress. Not even my elementary school productions wanted me."

He laughed as he pulled out of the parking space. "Just…be yourself," he said slowly. "How would you normally act around a boyfriend?"

"No idea. I've been responsible for my own orgasms for at least three years."

"I'd offer to help with that, but we just met, and after that much practice, you're probably far better at pleasing yourself than I would be."

Ha! "I can't decide if you're being honest or trying to convince me to let you try."

"Would I be an honest man if I said you were onto something with the last part of your sentence?"

"Yes, but as you said, we just met. And I'm only your fake girlfriend. Honestly, if you got me into bed, you might not let me out. That'd mess with this deception."

Mason laughed. "You think a lot about your bedroom skills, don't you?"

"Oh, I don't think anything. I know I'm great in bed. I've been the only one in mine that's been able to do anything right for years."

He banged a fist against his chest. "Well, of all the fake girlfriends I could have found, I'm glad it's you. Can you use some of that confidence to tell everyone how good in bed I am?"

"Why? Are you trying to pull someone? Jesus, way to dent my confidence." I flicked my hair over my shoulder and looked at him. "Is that how you treat your fake girlfriend?"

He quickly met my eyes. "You're something else. Do you know that?"

"Something else? What does that mean?" I paused. "If you mean a total delight, hilarious, a pleasure to be around, then you're right. Anything else, you're wrong, and we're going into this reunion on the tail end of a fight."

"Hey, at least that would be realistic."

"Yes, that's how you get under your ex's skin. You show up mid-fight with your fake girlfriend."

He burst into laughter and pulled up at the intersection.

"Do you know how ridiculous that sounds?"

I met his eyes. My only response was to laugh into my hand because he was so right. This entire situation was ridiculous, to be honest, but we had to make the best of it.

"Okay, we need to have our stories straight if we're going to pull this off," I said. "The problem is that my co-worker who I swapped shifts with thinks this is a date, so I need to clue her in just in case she says something."

"Right. We should go for a simple story." He put on the blinker and turned. "We can say we met online."

"Makes sense. App? Facebook? How?"

He grunted. "App?"

"Tinder? Two months ago?"

"That works."

"Perfect." I clapped my hands. "Now, what does your ex look like?"

"Doesn't matter. Knowing Claudia, she'll make an entrance." Mason made the turn to The Beachside. "She's dating her boss, and he's not exactly broke. She'll make a fuss."

Great. I was here to show up a diva. "Ugh. I'm the least dramatic person in the world."

"I don't know. You were pretty dramatic over my need for chicken wings."

"That's ridiculous." I rolled my eyes.

He put the car in park and grinned. "You really do have the exasperated girlfriend thing down. Are you sure we can't go in in the middle of a fight?"

"Mason, no. I can't pretend to both love you and be

mad at you. Jesus."

"A little more of that—"

"No." I laughed.

"Okay." He sighed. "Let's get this over with. How long do we have to stay?"

I got out of the car and shrugged. "Long enough for your ex to turn up and me to piss her off?"

He locked the car and rolled his shoulders. "I'm going to kill my sister for this shit."

"Mason!" A voice boomed across the parking lot.

He looked over his shoulder. "Shit—that's Trevor. He knows about this, just so you know."

"Oh, good. I don't have to act for another few minutes." I joined him at the back of his car as he greeted his friend.

Trevor was a little shorter than Mason but just as good-looking. Where were all these hot guys when I was actually looking for a date?

"Trev, this is Lauren. Lauren, this is Trevor." Mason waved between us.

Trevor looked me up and down with light brown eyes. "Well, shit, if you need a fake girlfriend…" He met my gaze, smirking. "It's a pleasure."

I smiled. "Nice to meet you."

He looked at Mason. "She's hotter than Claudia. She's going to flip her shit."

Mason shrugged. "That's her problem." He looked at me. "You ready to go in?"

Nodding, I took the arm he offered me by wrapping my

hand around the crook of his elbow. We walked toward the main doors of the bar with Trevor leading us in. He pushed open the door, holding it for us.

The second I stepped in, I immediately felt eyes on me. I knew exactly where they were coming from, and that was old Mr. Hennington at his usual spot at the bar.

He clutched a wrinkled, weathered hand to his face. "Lauren. You wound me."

I laughed. "Mr. Hennington, we've talked about this. Mrs. Lawrence would be devastated if we went out. I can't do that to her!"

"Oh, psh!" He waved his hand. "I've told you that she doesn't need to know about us."

"Stop tempting me." I wiggled my finger at him. "I'm not working tonight, and if you carry on with that, there's no telling what I'd do with you."

He chuckled, rocking his head side to side. "I don't think I'd survive the night, my darlin'."

I winked at him, waving at Pete behind the bar. "Exactly. Hey, Pete, is Stella out back?"

My boss nodded, cleaning a glass out. "Yep. And she's gonna want to talk to you." He looked pointedly at both Mason and Trevor.

"Oh, Pete, this is Mason, and this is Trevor. Guys, this is my boss and the owner of The Beachside, Pete."

"The owner?" Mason shook his hand when he leaned over the bar. "Do you know you seriously lack in chicken wings on your menu?"

"Fucking chicken wings," Trevor murmured.

I laughed, leaning into Mason's arm to mask it. It

seemed he felt the same way I did, and I'd bet he'd heard a hell of a lot more about it than I had.

"I happen to agree with you, son," Pete said. "Let me get the missus, and you can tell her. She's in charge of the food." He nodded toward the door that led to the kitchen. "Maybe she'll listen to someone who'll buy them. Until then, your party showed up early."

I nodded. "Come on," I said to both guys. "Let's go."

Here goes nothing.

CHAPTER FIVE

Mason

SHIT THE FUCKING BED, she was stunning.

That was all I could think as she stood over at the end of the bar, talking to the busty young woman on the other side of it. Lauren laughed, throwing her head back so her dark hair fell down her back in a shiny wave.

There was something about the bright pink of her dress that set off her gentle tan. It hung to just above her knees, and for my own sanity, I had to stop thinking about flipping the damn thing up and *her* over.

I rubbed my hand down my face and leaned against the wall. Trev came up beside me, holding out a beer. I curled my fingers around the neck of the ice-cold bottle and, with a nod of thanks, took a deep pull of beer.

"How the fuck," Trev started, "did she come out of an online ad?"

I shook my head. "Dunno. She only put it up for a joke because her friends and sister made her."

"At least you have something in common. Doing shit because your sister makes you."

I snorted and wiped my mouth. "No shit. That's the reason I'm here in the first place."

"She's hot enough to turn a fake date to a real one, though."

"I'm not interested in dating anyone right now. You know that." I swigged again.

"Are you telling me she doesn't change your mind?" He pointed in her direction before I slapped his hand down. "She'd change my fucking mind. Hell, I want to date her. Can I have her if you don't want her?"

"Can you have her? Fucking hell, Trev, she's not a leftover slice of cake."

He grinned. "Yeah, but could you imagine if she was?"

I shook my head. I wasn't going to go down whatever road he was steering me toward.

Yes, Lauren was hot as fuck. Yes, she was the kind of girl I could see myself taking out again.

No, I wasn't going to make this fake date real.

I wasn't ready to date anyone. That wasn't me being a salty asshole because of Claudia, but it was the truth. I was happy the way I was right now.

No matter how attracted I was to Lauren Green.

Maybe a one-night stand was an option. Maybe she'd be in agreement with that. After all, that benefitted us both.

Shit, no—what was I thinking? I couldn't walk up to

the woman and say, "Hey, I don't want to see you again, but let's fuck."

Jesus Christ.

I was spending too much time around Trevor.

Lauren laughed, picking up her wine glass from the bar, and touched the arm of the girl behind the bar. She skirted the outside of the room as she made her way over to me and sidled up next to me.

"Sorry about that," she said quietly. "This was supposed to be my shift and, well, Stella's a nosy bitch."

I may have met her anyway? Fucking hell. The sad part was I probably wouldn't have paid the blindest bit of attention to her if she were behind the bar.

Shit, it didn't matter what attention I paid to her.

We were pretending. This wasn't a real date. This was her…well, I still wasn't sure what the hell either of us were doing with this stupid arrangement, but I was mostly getting Kirsty off my back at this point.

"No worries." I stood a little straighter. "We don't have to stay long."

Lauren shrugged one shoulder. "It's your reunion. I'm just here to look pretty."

"And you're doing an awesome job of it," Trev inputted. "Now, talk to me about Stella. Is she single?"

I pressed my fingers into my temples. Trev was my best friend, but my God, the guy thought with his dick a little too often.

Lauren touched her fingertips to her mouth as she bit back a laugh. "She's single," she confirmed. "But she'll eat you for breakfast."

"I don't mind being breakfast. I'll be lunch and dinner, too, if she'll let me."

This time, she didn't hide her laugh. "Oh, my God. That line is awful."

"It's not a line. It's the truth."

She looked at me. "He's joking, right?"

Grimacing, I met her eyes. "I wish I could say he was. He's what kids today call a fuckboy."

"It's not just the kids. He's definitely a fuckboy."

My lips twitched. "Really? My sister just calls him a cu—"

"Incoming, three o'clock," Trev interrupted me, giving me a nudge with his elbow.

I knew what I'd see before I turned my head.

Claudia.

She strolled through the door on the arm of her boss. Her long, blonde hair was curled over one shoulder and hung to almost her waist in curls. The black dress she wore hugged her body from the neck to her knees, and she carried a clearly expensive purse that was slung over her shoulder.

Her dark blue eyes scanned the room at the same time Lauren tucked herself beneath my arm and pressed her body against mine. Her fingers grazed my hip as she looped her arm around my waist. "Is that your ex?"

She'd clearly heard Trev's interruption. Not that it was hard. The dead could hear Trevor.

"Yeah," I said, loosely resting my arm over her shoulders. "That's Claudia."

"And her boss," Trev coughed into his hand.

Lauren brought her fingers to her mouth. "Really? That's her boss?"

I glanced at the man who had at least twenty years on us, as evidenced by his gray-dotted beard. "Yeah. She's a paralegal, and he owns the law firm where she works. I, uh, got a front-row seat to that little show."

Her eyes widened as my meaning caught on. "Oh, shit. Do you think she'll come over here?"

"Yes," I said honestly. "She's just that kind of person."

Lauren adjusted her body position and discreetly tugged at her dress.

"What are you doing?"

She peered up at me. "What any good fake girlfriend does. I'm adjusting my dress so my boobs look extra good."

I couldn't help but laugh at her. She was so nonchalant, so confident, like it didn't bother her at all that my raging bitch of an ex was across the room.

Mind you, it probably didn't.

There was no reason for it to bother her. She just had to act like it did. I probably should have checked on her acting ability before I agreed to do this…

Claudia's eyes scanned the entire room yet again before they settled on me with a self-satisfied smirk. She held my gaze for a long minute before Lauren moved, apparently drawing her attention because her gaze dropped.

Lauren leaned up, bringing her mouth to my ear. "My cat would shit on her head if he saw her."

I laughed, dropping my chin to my chest, but not before I saw the smirk disappear from Claudia's face. "Your cat would shit on her head?"

"Yeah. Henry has an obsession with sitting on people's heads. He thinks humans are his own personal bean bag, but he'd literally use her as his litter box."

"He sounds like an asshole."

"A total asshole. Means he's a good judge of character."

"How does that make sense?"

"Because he doesn't give a flying fuck about offending anyone."

"He's a cat. How can he offend anyone?"

"Have you ever had a cat sit on your head and fart?"

"I can't say that's something I've ever experienced, no."

She nodded. "I wouldn't recommend it."

"Noted." My lips twitched as I glanced up. Claudia had moved to the bar with her boss-slash-boyfriend and was deep in conversation with a girl she'd been close with in high school. Her attention kept darting this way, though, and I held her gaze for a second before I looked away.

"You all right?" Trev asked, eyes flicking toward Lauren.

I shrugged. "Honestly, I am. I don't feel a damn thing toward her."

"And your girlfriend is happy to hear it," Lauren chirped. "Now, how long do we have until she inevitably comes over here and starts questioning me?"

"You'll be fine," I said. "We have our story straight, as long as Trev shuts his mouth."

"Trust me," he said dryly, lifting his beer. "The second Satan herself comes over here, I'm going to take a leak."

"Lovely."

♥

He didn't have to wait long to take his piss. Whether he even needed to go or not was a question for another day, but Claudia had barely said hello to three people before Lauren prodded me in the back, making me look up.

She had her hand wrapped around the crook of her boss' elbow, but she was the one dragging him across the room like a woman on a mission. Which she was.

A mission to make my life a living hell.

For his part, her boss looked like he'd rather be anywhere other than here. Not only walking toward us, but in the room entirely. He had at least ten years on the rest of us, and I knew Claudia well enough to know that he was here just for her to flaunt him.

God only knew the man probably had better things to do than be here. Hell, I did, and I didn't have my own business. I only "built walls and shit," as she'd so nicely said to me when she'd removed her legs from around his waist.

"Brace yourself," Trev muttered. He downed the rest of his beer and stalked off without even acknowledging Claudia's existence.

Claudia pursed her lips and flicked her hair over her shoulder. "He's still as rude as ever, I see."

That was a matter of opinion. "Claudia. How are you?" I asked tightly.

The smile that crept across her face was sly and self-satisfied. "Better than ever. How are you?"

"Couldn't be better," I replied. "Have you met Lauren?"

Claudia turned her attention to Lauren for half a second. "I didn't know you were seeing anyone."

"You didn't realize you were seeing me for a while, either, so I don't know why you'd care about who I'm seeing now."

Lauren twitched, bringing her glass to her lips.

"I don't care," Claudia said, shrugging one shoulder. "I was merely making conversation."

"Then make it somewhere else," I said dryly. "You're only here to attempt to rub your relationship in my face, and since that isn't going to work, I'm sure there's someone else here who'll pretend to be suitably impressed to feed your ego."

Her expression froze before anger flashed in her eyes.

Bingo. I'd hit the nail on the head and hammered it right in.

"I came over to be polite and see how you are." She pushed her hair from her eyes and resumed her holier-than-thou look.

"Well, now you've seen," Lauren said brightly. "You've made conversation and know he's just fine. I don't see that you have much else to talk about considering you aren't bothering to introduce your date. But, oh wait, that would be awkward, wouldn't it, since they've already met?"

Claudia's lips pursed. "And you'd know all about that, would you?"

Lauren shrugged. "Enough that I can't decide if you're brave or stupid, given the last time you all saw each other, your date was balls deep inside you. Looks like he left them in your purse, too."

Well, shit.

Claudia took a step forward, but Lauren didn't even twitch. Instead of reacting to Claudia's intimidation tactics, she sipped her wine, smiled, and looked at Claudia's date.

"No offense," she added in a chirpy tone.

He looked thoroughly unamused, his eyes darkening as he focused on her for a moment. "Claudia, let's go."

"I—"

He didn't give her a chance to finish her reply before he took control of the situation and spun them around, sweeping her away before she could do any more damage.

Lauren tilted her head to the side. "You know, if we were monkeys, she'd be the kind of person I'd fling my poop at."

The mouthful of beer I'd just taken shot straight up my nose and burned, and she pulled away, biting her bottom lip.

"Sorry." She tried to hide her giggles. "For what it's worth, she'd probably fling it at me, too."

I bashed my fist against my chest and nodded. "You're probably right. Also, this whole thing was worth it just to see you shoot her down like that."

Lauren sighed. "I'm a woman. I've had years of dealing with bitches. I deal with one on a regular basis."

"You do?"

"Yeah. Myself." She paused. "We're all bitches. Some of us just hide it a little better than others, which is why it's a surprise when we let the bitch flag fly high."

I raised my eyebrow, smirking. "Was that you letting your bitch flag fly high?"

"Oh, no. That thing was only waving at half-mast. If it was fully up there, she'd be on the way to the emergency room to get treated for some burns I'd deliver."

Right. Because she hadn't already done that.

She smiled brightly before holding out her glass. "Could you please hold this for a second? I need to use the restroom."

"I'll hold your hair while you throw up after that performance." I took the glass from her. "And I'm not even kidding."

Laughing, she turned on her toes and stalked away, sweeping her hair around to one side of her neck. She glanced back at me with a little grin before she disappeared between two small groups of people.

Slowly, I shook my head.

She was beautiful, funny, *and* had the ultimate take-no-shit attitude.

Jesus.

If this date were real, I'd be fucked seven ways to Sunday.

"Why do you look like you just fell in love?" Trev reappeared with a beer in his hand. "Where did Satan go?"

I snorted. "Lauren ran her off. Literally. She told her that we were done talking here because the last time we saw each other, her nameless boyfriend was balls-deep in her and that he'd left his balls in her purse. He dragged Claudia off before she could start a fight."

"Well, shit," he breathed. "Seriously, if you're not going to date this girl for real, I'm gonna."

"No, you're not," I said firmly. "Just because I'm not dating her doesn't mean you can."

"Why not?"

"Because she's too good for you, you pervert. That's why."

Trev sighed. "Think Kirsty will find me a hot fake date like her?"

Laughing, I leaned back against the wall and said, "I don't think there *is* another fake date like her."

CHAPTER SIX

Lauren

WE'D BOTH ONLY had one drink each, so by the time we left the bar an hour later, both me and Mason were two things: hungry and thirsty.

Instead of hanging around and risking running into Claudia again, we got into his truck and headed for the one place you could always count on being there for you.

McDonald's.

That's right. Our fake date was officially over, technically, and McDonald's was the last place you'd ever take a girl on a date if you were over the age of fifteen.

So to McDonald's we went. Honestly, the idea of a double cheeseburger had me almost drooling over his dashboard. I was so ready to load up on carbs and regret it the next time I tried to put skinny jeans on.

It took us only a few minutes to get from the bar to the

restaurant, and Mason slowed as we entered the parking lot. "Eat in or use the drive-thru?"

"Drive-thru," I said without thinking. "There are people inside."

Laughing, he changed gear and moved the car into the lane for the drive-thru. "Do you know what you're having?"

"Does a bear shit in the woods? This is McDonald's, man, not a fancy steakhouse. Everyone knows what they're getting when they come to this place."

"True. Sometimes I change it up, though. Big Mac or a cheeseburger?"

"Both good," I replied as we moved forward. "Depends if you fancy something cheesy or saucy."

He flashed me an amused look, lips twitching to the side. "Well, I've got saucy in the next seat, so I guess cheesy."

A laugh exploded from me. "Saucy? Really? I don't think anyone has ever called me saucy in my life."

"Ah, well, you're bold and flippant, so that means you're saucy."

"Ooh. Handsome, unavailable, and a smarty-pants. Aren't you a walking temptation for women?"

It was Mason's turn to laugh—and he did. Hard. "That's only half of it. You should—"

"Hello, what can I get for you?" The voice boomed through the speaker, startling us both.

"Shit," he hissed. "Uh, hi, I'll have a large Big Mac meal with a Coke and… Uh, Lauren?"

"I'll have a medium double cheeseburger meal, two

servings of bacon, extra cheese, add ketchup, but hold the pickles, mustard, tomato, onion, and lettuce, and a strawberry milkshake, please," I rattled off my regular order.

What? I was a fussy eater. As in, I liked my junk food without vegetables or salad.

"All right, move through to the window, please."

Mason eyed me as he did just that. "Really? Is ordering a burger that complicated?"

I shrugged a shoulder. "I'm picky. About burgers, underwear, and men."

"Three valid things to be picky about," he said, amusement tingeing his tone. "Has anyone ever told you that you're something else?"

"Yes, but it's usually not a good something." I side-eyed him.

"This is a good something. If this date were real and I had any intention of actually dating for real, I'd say this was a successful one."

I held up my hand for a high-five. "I agree. Except for the altercation with the ex, that is. I wouldn't advise that for a future first date. Or any kind of date, really."

"Completely agree. I'd avoid it otherwise, too." Mason pulled his wallet from his pocket.

"I can pay mine."

"No, you're good. Think of this as a thank you for letting my sister rope you into this nonsense." He handed his card through the window before I could argue. "And I know you were partially to blame, but still. You didn't have to agree."

I made a noise that he could take as either dissension

or agreement. I wanted to pay my way because this wasn't a real date and I was stubborn, but a free cheeseburger was a free cheeseburger, and I wasn't going to turn one down.

Yes, I was, in fact, in a serious relationship with food.

It was always there for you. Good news, bad news, no news—it was a loyalty I could get behind.

We rolled forward to the next window and waited. Our drinks were handed to us, and we pulled up into one of the parking spots allocated for the drive-thru.

"I miss the plastic straws," Mason said, eyeing the cardboard one in his hand.

"You ever tried to drink a milkshake through one of these? It's like sucking the soul from a devil," I replied, shoving the cardboard straw into the cup and showing him exactly what I meant. My cheeks were completely hollowed out by the time I got my first mouthful of frozen shake.

Mason stared at me for a moment. "You have one hell of a way with words."

"I'd bow, but there's a dashboard in the way." I grinned. "And thank you. It's one of the things I pride myself on."

He chuckled, putting his drink in the holder. "You know, this could have gone so much worse. I didn't want to do this at all, but now a part of me is glad I did."

"Only because I took your ex's stiletto and stuck it up her ass."

"For all intents and purposes, yes, but what other reason would there be?"

At that moment, the McDonald's worker appeared and handed the bag full of food to Mason. He passed it to me so he could reverse out of the waiting spot and pull into one of the regular spaces.

I split the food. "I don't know," I said. "My stunning personality? My quick wit? How great this dress makes my boobs look?"

His eyes drifted down to my chest.

"Hey. Up here." I snapped my fingers.

He jerked his eyes up. "Look, you basically offered me a glance there. I was taking it."

I rolled my eyes. "Whatever. So this night was good because I shot down your ex and my boobs look good in this dress. I'm not as bothered by that as you'd think."

I'd had worse real dates, never mind fake ones.

"Well, if it makes your night better, Trev wants to date you for real." He took a huge bite out of his burger.

Me?

Well, I choked on my fry. "I'm sorry, what?"

Mason wiped the corner of his mouth with his hand and swallowed. "He said that if I didn't want you, could he have you?"

"I'm not the last pre-packed sandwich at the store." Fucking men. "Besides, wasn't he asking about Stella?"

"Yeah, but just in case it wasn't glaringly obvious, he's a fucking man whore."

"Really," I drawled, grabbing a few fries and dipping them in my ketchup. "I couldn't tell."

Mason glanced at me sideways. "So I can definitely tell him no?"

"You can definitely tell him no," I confirmed. "I'm all

good there, thanks. I don't want to date anyone right now."

"You and me both."

"Well, any fake date that contains a bit of bitchiness to an ex and ends with a cheeseburger is worth my time." I met his eyes and grinned, raising my milkshake. "Cheers."

He tapped his Coke against my cup. "I'll drink to that."

♥

Yawning, I spooned a can of wet food into Henry's ceramic dish. He sniffed it for a minute before he turned away and stalked into the living room.

Fussy little shit.

I put the can aside to recycle and tossed the spoon, then washed my hands before I turned on the coffee machine. Nobody needed their coffee cup to smell like cat food. I slid my mug asking, "Does running out of fucks count as cardio?" beneath the machine, then I hit the button for it to go and eyed the gray smudge of cat as Henry quietly plodded across the kitchen.

I shook my head.

He was fussy, but he was still hungry. And a cat, which meant he was a pain in the ass by default.

I took my cup from the coffee machine and poured in some cream before I added a lump of sugar. While I hadn't stayed out late last night for my fake date, it honestly felt like it'd lasted forever.

Or maybe that was just the part where I'd gotten a little too into being Mason's girlfriend and shot his ex down.

Look—it's already well established that I'm not perfect. I'm not always the best at thinking before I speak, and sometimes, I battle bitchiness with bitchiness.

Yes, yes, you can catch more flies with honey than with vinegar, but I don't want to catch flies.

I want to swat them.

Which was exactly what I did with Claudia last night. I swatted her bitchy little behind until Mr. No-Balls took her away before she made a fool of herself. Well, a bigger fool than she already had.

That had happened the second she'd thought it was a good idea to go and talk to Mason.

I blew out a deep breath and put some bread in the toaster. Thank God it was over and not my problem anymore, meaning that Claudia wasn't either.

She was hard work.

That didn't mean I was fully against everything. Actually, in a weird way, I was a little gutted I wouldn't see Mason again. He was exactly the kind of guy I would have picked off a dating app—which meant it was probably a good thing I wouldn't see him again, given my disastrous track record.

Still, we'd had a fun time. At least, I'd had one. Not only was he hot as hell, but he made me laugh, and we'd gotten along really well, in my opinion.

Shit happened, though. He wasn't ready for a relationship, and I didn't blame him. Claudia cheating on him aside, she struck me as the kind of woman who had the mentality of, "I don't want him, but you can't have him, either." Getting into a relationship would probably be more hassle than it was worth for him.

And that was fine by me. I didn't particularly want one

right now either—some people were happy being single, thank you very much. Even if I did want a relationship, I most definitely didn't want one that came with a pain in the ass ex.

I already had my sister and two best friends to be that for me. I didn't need anyone else's problem.

My toast popped and I pulled it out to butter it while it was still hot. When it was done, I picked up one slice and leaned against the counter, looking out of the window.

It wasn't much of a view. Half a brick wall and some trees that occasionally gave me an elusive glimpse at the Gulf of Mexico wasn't much to write home about, but sometimes, swaying leaves were calming.

Ugh. I was too poetic this morning. This was why I didn't go on dates. They made you mushy and shit—and I was not mushy. I was not baby food, even if I did enjoy the odd spoonful of applesauce.

My grandma made a boss applesauce.

I was getting off track.

The morning was beautiful. The kind of morning that sadistic directors in romantic comedy movies ruined by sending stupid texts or having an idiot knock at the door. You know, that stereotypical bullshit where the birds were singing and the sun was shi—

And three knocks sounded at the door.

I almost dropped my coffee cup.

"I have carbs!" Madi's voice was muffled as she knocked again.

Ah-ha.

There was the idiot who knocked at the door.

"What kind of carbs?" I shouted back.

"All of them!"

I'd take it. "It's open!"

"Ugh." Madi shoved the door open. "You made me stand there like an idiot, why?"

I shrugged and grabbed another coffee cup, this one emblazoned with the phrase, "This is probably alcohol," to make Madi a drink. "It was for my own amusement. You're awake early."

"Ugh," she repeated, tucking her hair behind her ear. "The couple upstairs were having a blazing row at six a.m., so I went for a run and decided to come over here." She set a big, brown paper bag with my favorite bakery's logo on the side on the island and slid onto a stool. "How did your non-date go last night?"

I groaned, pushing her coffee toward her. "He was beautiful, Madi. It was as though he'd walked right out of a wet dream and materialized at my door."

She choked on her mouthful of coffee. "All right, then. And the rest?"

I gave her a quick run-down of the evening before launching into my rant about Claudia. "Honestly, she's the kind of person you'd throw your shoe at. I swear to God; she'd make a saint contemplate murder. She was just… catty."

"And you sound like a regular nice girl right now."

"Oh, come on. I'm not always a bitch."

"Only days that end in 'y', right?"

"Right." I dove my hand into the bakery bag and pulled out individually packed pastries. "But I'm, like, your friendly neighborhood bitch. I'm here for your side-eyes and your resting bitch face and the occasional catty comment. She's the smug bitch who saunters around on a horse so high that, when she falls, she'll hit the ground so hard that she'll go straight to hell."

Madi took a pastry, laughing. "You're right. You are the friendly neighborhood bitch. You should put that on one of your beloved mugs."

I glanced at my cupboard full of slogan mugs. "I might just do that."

"Right, while you order that, tell me more about Mason. He sounds like a snack and a half." She tore her croissant in half and waved one half at me. "He's the kind of guy I'd like to lick up and down with—"

"Yeah, yeah," I replied. "I know. He is. Honestly, if I wanted to date, then he'd be the perfect guy. But I don't, so he isn't." I pulled my own buttered croissant out from the bag. Screw the toast I'd eaten—there was no such thing as too many bread products. "Besides, did I mention his ex cheated on him? He said he doesn't want a relationship."

"And you're totally fine with all that?"

"Mad, I went on the date because you, Tina, and Iz made me. You guys are the only reason I ever put that bullshit ad up." I held up a bit of my croissant. "Without that, it never would have happened. Was Mason hot? Yes. Was I attracted to him? Yes. I can move on and live my life perfectly fine without ripping off his pants and riding his penis like a motorized bull."

That's what dirty dreams and vibrators were for.

"Can you?" Madi asked. "Because that was pretty intense."

"Oh, my God, yes." Laughing, I wiped my mouth and picked up my coffee. "Look, I know nothing about the guy. I literally spent the night looking pretty and talking about, well, I don't even know. But it's not like we were gazing into each other's eyes over a steak dinner. We had fucking McDonald's as a post-reunion snack. In his car."

She burst out laughing. "That's the most Lauren thing ever. Fancy dinner? Nah. Let's go to the McD's drive-thru, order a cheeseburger, and eat in your car. Perfect first date."

I held up a hand. "Look, if a man can't take me eating a cheeseburger in his passenger seat, he doesn't deserve me eating his dick in his bedroom."

She coughed violently and thumped her fist against her chest. I went to help her, but she motioned for water, so I grabbed a bottle from the fridge and uncapped it before I handed it to her.

She downed several mouthfuls of it before she set it on the countertop and looked at me. "I take the friendly neighborhood bitch thing back. Put *that* on a mug."

I grinned, tearing a second croissant in two. "I'll put that on a flag and fly it from my window if I have to."

Madi shook her head. "This is why you're single. The only filter you use is on Instagram."

"We're not all proficient in Photoshop," I shot back. "And I'm single because I want to be, thank you very much."

She snorted. "Are you telling me that if this Mason guy called you tomorrow and asked you on another date that you'd say no?"

"Absolutely," I said without missing a beat. "I swear to God, I wouldn't do it. I cannot imagine a scenario where

I would ever, ever, put myself in the line of fire of his ex again. I'd rather eat my own nipples for breakfast."

"Are you sure?"

"One thousand percent," I said firmly. "Now, let's find you a date instead."

CHAPTER SEVEN

Mason

*I*F THERE WAS ANYTHING I dreaded more than having dinner with my parents and my mother asking when I'd start dating again, it was my Grandpa Ernie being there and telling me about all the women *he was dating*.

Mostly because I didn't need the mental image of my eighty-year-old grandfather getting it on, but partly because my mom side-eyed me every single time.

If my grandpa could get over losing his wife of sixty years and date other women, I could move on from Claudia.

She didn't seem to understand that I had moved on from her. I just wanted to be single.

It made dinner… interesting.

Which was why I was taking my sweet-ass time driving home from work. With any luck, my mom would be so pissed I was late that she wouldn't bother talking about my dating life—unless my sister brought it up.

Which she probably would, so I'd bring up hers right back.

Sure, Kirsty was actively dating, but she was picking total assholes.

Begrudgingly, I pulled up outside my apartment block and headed upstairs. I'd just put my key in the lock when the door behind me swung open.

"Good afternoon, Mrs. Allerton," I said politely, pushing my door and turning around.

"Is it?" She sniffed. "There was someone knocking at your door earlier."

I should have guessed. "I'm really sorry if they disturbed you."

Another sniff. "You should tell your female callers that they need to call before they stop by and interrupt Maury."

"I will do just that," I reassured her. "Do you happen to know who it was?"

"No. Maury had the DNA results."

"How do you know it was a woman if you didn't see them?"

"I might have looked through my peephole," she admitted after a minute. "They had a hood up, but it looked like a woman. I told her that I'd shoot her if she didn't stop hammering away."

Tilting my head slightly, I said, "You don't own a gun."

"You're right, I don't." She knocked her cane against the floor. "But your floozies don't know that, do they?"

I gave her a tight smile. It was no use trying to tell her that I didn't have any "floozies," as she put it. She'd just argue the toss with me. It'd taken me eighteen months to convince her that Kirsty was my sister.

"Absolutely not. I'll pass your messages on."

"Thank you. Don't you have to get ready for dinner with your family?"

Ah, small towns and nosy neighbors. Who'd live anywhere else?

"Yes, ma'am, I do. I'm actually a little late."

"Then why are you still standing here talking to me?" She sniffed and turned around. "Kids these days. So disrespectful."

I took a deep breath and went into my apartment before she'd shut her door. Telling her that I was twenty-eight and not exactly a child wouldn't work in my favor and just start a whole long rant about not arguing with my elders.

I already had my grandfather to deal with tonight. One pensioner was more than enough for today.

I tossed my phone and keys onto the kitchen island and pulled my shirt over my head on the way to the bathroom. It fell to the floor, but ignored it to pick up later, and instead focused on the shower.

I washed the dirt and dust from the building site away from my body and got back out. I really didn't have long to get changed, so I gave my hair a quick rub with the towel and got dressed, leaving it still damp as I headed back out the door.

Hopefully, no "floozies" would come knocking at my door when I was out.

I pulled up behind Kirsty's car in my parents' driveway. I was already regretting coming here, but not quite as much as I did when the front door swung open before I'd even gotten out of my truck.

"Mason Jackson!" my mother snapped. "You're late."

I took a deep breath and got out. "Hello to you, too, Mom."

"Hello," she replied. "You're still late."

"Sorry. I was late finishing work. You didn't wait, did you?"

"Everyone except your grandfather." She accepted my kiss on the cheek and moved aside so I could get in. "You know what he's like."

I did. The man would eat his own fingers if you didn't feed him. A bit like a hungry toddler.

In fact, old people had a lot in common with toddlers—at least in my experience. They needed help visiting the bathroom, got grumpy when they were hungry, and said your name repeatedly until you answered.

Or maybe that was just Grandpa Ernie.

Who was currently slurping spaghetti while wearing a napkin as a bib.

Yep. He was an overgrown toddler.

"What's up, Grandpa?" I asked, joining everyone at the table. "Hey, Dad, Kirsty."

"Hey, son. How was work?" Dad asked, looking up from the paper he was reading. "Still down at the old

Hawkins place?"

I nodded, reaching for some bread as Mom put a steaming plate of spaghetti in front of me. "We're putting the roof on the new barn now. We should be done with it by next week."

"How's Sam?"

"As ornery as ever," Kirsty replied before I could. "I was out there yesterday to interview him about the market to see if he'd be bringing some of his produce, and he told me to have my people call his people."

I eyed her. "You're the junior reporter. You *are* the newspaper's people."

She stuck her tongue out at me, earning herself a quick slap around the back of the head from Mom.

"Let's say grace." Mom clasped her hands together, forcing all of us—except Grandpa—to do the same. "Lord, we thank you for this food you blessedly provided us, and I hope that you send a nice young lady the way of my son. Amen."

Yeah, and hopefully she was Australian.

"I don't think he's listening, Nadia," Grandpa Ernie said, pausing to slurp on a long piece of spaghetti. "You've been praying to the man upstairs for a girlfriend for Mason every day for three months, and he's still single."

"That's by choice, Grandpa. Not even God can override free will," I said. "Much to Mom's displeasure."

"He has a point, honey," Dad said, grabbing a piece of garlic bread from the plate in the middle of the table. "You can lead a horse to water, but you can't make it drink. You could put Mason in the middle of a speed dating circuit, and he'd still not find anyone he wanted to date."

"You're saying it like I'm taking up the vow of a priest." I grabbed my own bit of garlic bread and split it in two. "I don't know how many times we have to have this conversation."

"Until you meet someone, darling," Mom said as if it was the simplest thing in the world.

"I'm not the only single one here, you know. Kirsty's single."

"Yes, but she's three years younger than you."

"Give the kid a break, Nadia," Grandpa Ernie said, wiping his mouth with a napkin and reaching for his whiskey. "He's only twenty-eight. Men don't have alarm clocks in their genitals like you women."

I spat out my water, and my sister did the same.

Mom looked wide-eyed at him. "Dad! That's inappropriate for the dinner table!"

He cackled. He'd said it deliberately because he knew it would rile her, and that was mission accomplished.

"Actually," Kirsty said. "I do have some news on the dating front."

I raised my eyebrow at her. "You're dating someone? Do I need to send him my condolences?"

Mom shot me a glare before turning to her. "You're dating?"

"No." Kirsty snorted. "But Mason is. He's just not telling you."

I froze as four pairs of eyes all landed on me. What the fuck was she playing—

Oh, no.

She was not going to bring up Lauren, was she?

I met her eyes. They glinted. She was. She fucking was.

"Kirsty, shut up," I said, teeth gritted.

"You're dating?" Mom's head jerked between the two of us until she made even me feel dizzy. "Who is she? Is it serious? How long has this been going on?"

"Nadia, calm down," Dad said. "If he doesn't want to share, he doesn't want to share."

"I'll share," Kirsty piped in.

"No, you won't." I glared at her.

"Her name is Lauren. They met not long ago, and he took her to his reunion on Friday." The words escaped her so quickly that it took everyone a moment to catch up with what she'd said.

I was going to kill her.

Slowly and fucking painfully.

"Is she hot?" Grandpa Ernie asked, licking his fingers as he fixed his dark blue eyes on me.

"Dad!" Mom admonished. "Mason, why didn't you tell us you were seeing this girl?"

"Because he's a grown man and he can keep parts of his life to himself," Dad drawled. "I know that's a foreign concept to you, honey, but it's a thing."

"Well, I'm not saying I need a play-by-play! But it would be nice to meet this young lady."

"He'll introduce us if and when he wants to." Dad poured more water in his glass. "Don't pressure him or he'll run off and never speak to us again."

That was tempting right now.

"No, he won't. I'm not out of line by asking about her."

"Is she hot?" Grandpa repeated, ignoring their bickering. "I don't blame you keeping her secret if she's hot. I'm a bit of a stud. Are you worried she'll run off with me instead?"

The napkin that peeked out of his sweater was coated in spaghetti sauce, and so was his mouth. "Yes, Grandpa, that's it. I'm worried she'll be swept off her feet by your handsome self."

"I knew it."

"Well?" Mom said, nudging me. "Will we meet her soon? How serious is it?"

I looked at Kirsty. She had a sickening smug look on her face, and if we were teenagers, I'd be wiping it off her face with a headlock. She had no idea what a clusterfuck she'd just created with her stupid little joke. It was one thing to mess with me, but to mess with someone she didn't even know—that was low.

Maybe if I could play down the so-called seriousness of it all, then I could hold off my mom until Lauren and I "broke up." That was about the only option I had right now.

"It's new," I said cautiously. "I don't think introducing her to the family just yet is a good idea."

"Why not?" Mom said. "Better she knows what she's getting into. It's your grandpa's birthday this weekend. Why don't you bring her to the party?"

Grandpa shimmied in his seat. "More bitches for Ernie!"

Kirsty choked on her spaghetti.

Dad leaned over and took the glass of whiskey. "I think we'll switch this for water."

"I think not," I said to Mom. "I can't think of anything worse."

"I can think of plenty of things that are worse than introducing your new girlfriend to your family. Poverty. No clean water. Malaria."

"All right, I get it, I get it." I rubbed my hand down my face. "We'll see. She might have to work."

"If she's working during the party, she can come to dinner on Thursday night. How does that sound?"

Like I'd rather put my balls in a blender.

"We'll see," I repeated. I was not going to agree to anything that I'd regret later.

Although, I had a feeling that this was one battle I'd already lost.

♥

I grabbed Kirsty before she could get into her car. "What the fuck are you playing at?"

She yanked her arm away from me and smirked. "You had fun with her. What's the harm in one more date?"

"A ton of harm," I said bitterly. "Just because we had a good time doesn't mean that either of us wants to have a relationship. I don't know what you're playing at, but it's bullshit."

"Look, just text her. See if she'll go with you."

"I can't."

"Sure you can. It's one message, Mase."

"No, I can't." I shook my head. "I deleted her number and our texts. I can't contact her."

She stared at me for a moment. "Good thing I still have it, isn't it?"

"You're kidding me."

"Nope." She grinned. "Pass me your phone."

"This is a fucking terrible idea."

"I know. It's why I suggested it. Gimme." She wiggled her fingers, and I reluctantly handed her the phone out of my pocket. She tapped on the screen and showed me it. She'd added Lauren's number to my contacts. "There. Just text her and see what she says."

I snatched my phone back. "I'm gonna kill you for this, you know that?"

She shrugged and unlocked her car. "You can try, but we both know you're gonna send this message."

"Doesn't mean I'm not gonna kill you." I flipped her the bird before I got into my truck and backed onto the street so she could get out. She beeped her horn at me and shot me an annoyingly cheery wave out of the window before she drove down the street.

I stared at my phone.

This was insane. But I didn't really have a choice. Kirsty had well and truly shoved me into the deep end with this.

MASON: Hey, can we talk?

I'd driven home by the time her response came through.

LAUREN: Who's this?

MASON: Mason.

LAUREN: Oh, right, sorry. I didn't keep your number. What's up?

MASON: Nothing to worry about, but I need to talk to you. Are you free now?

LAUREN: I'm at work. My break is nearly over and we're slammed. Is it important?

MASON: Not really. It can wait.

LAUREN: I start work at six tomorrow. Why don't you come in then? We can talk there.

MASON: Sounds good. I'll come straight from work.

LAUREN: Okay, see you then.

Fuck.

CHAPTER EIGHT

Lauren

*C*AN WE TALK?

Those were three words no girl wanted to hear from a guy, no matter the status of their relationship. They were most certainly not words you wanted to hear from a guy you'd fake-dated one time.

Yet, here I was, at work, waiting for Mason to come in here. I'd be lying if I said I wasn't a little nervous about this conversation. I'd even go as far to say as I had butterflies, but I'd say it damn reluctantly.

I had nothing. I'd been rolling his words over and over in my mind ever since I'd gotten his text yesterday. The only thing I could think of was that he wanted to take me out for real.

I wasn't against that, for the record. But I wasn't for it, either. I really was happy being single, and I really didn't want the baggage of a crazy ex-girlfriend when I did date again.

Of course, I was a woman, which meant I'd dissected that thought seven ways to Sunday. I'd driven myself crazy thinking about why he wanted to talk to the point I'd even broken a glass before my shift had started.

"You're away with the fairies, Lauren."

I jerked my attention away from the door and toward one of our regulars, an old veteran. "I sure am, Randy. Sorry about that. You want your usual?"

"Don't you worry about me, girl. I'd wager the fairies have a prettier world than we do." He winked. "Yes, the usual, if you don't mind."

"No problem." I grabbed a glass and moved to the Guinness tap. "How's Belinda?" I asked, referring to his wife who'd recently broken her ankle.

"She's doin' good. Going crazy with some cabin fever, so the daughter's taken her out to get a bite to eat with the grandkids. Do her some good, I reckon."

"You're probably right there. Send her my love, and make sure you bring her in here instead of creeping away for a beer every day." I jokingly wiggled my finger at him as I slid him the beer.

Laughing, he handed me a five-dollar bill. "If you don't tell her about this one, you can keep the change."

I winked. "You'll tell me to keep it anyway."

Another laugh. "Damn it, I'm not as mysterious as I think I am."

I slid his change across the bar to him anyway. "Not at all, Randy, not at all."

With a wink, he pushed the change back to me. "Did

81

you know there's a nice young man at the other end of the bar staring at you?"

I looked over my shoulder. Mason was standing at the other end of the bar, dust in his dark hair and on his pale blue polo shirt. His lips twitched up when he saw me.

"I do now," I said to Randy. "And don't you start." I pointed my finger at him.

He grinned and leaned around me. "She's single, you know!"

"Away with you!" I grabbed a cloth and flicked it in his direction. His laughter echoed through the bar as he headed to his table in the corner to do his crossword puzzle.

Shaking my head, I glanced quickly around the bar to make sure nobody needed anything and walked down to Mason.

"You've got some characters in here." His lips twitched.

"You have no idea," I said dryly. "Can I get you a drink?"

"Sure, why not? I'll have a Coors."

"Coming right up." I turned and pulled one from one of the low fridges. Uncapping it, I set it on the bar mat in front of him and said, "Two-eighty, please."

I took the five-dollar bill he handed me and rang up his order. Going back to join him, I handed him the change before I held up my finger so I could serve the couple who'd just joined the bar.

A couple of minutes later, I rejoined Mason. "Sorry. What did you need to talk about?"

"You sure you can talk?"

"Yeah, if you don't mind me running off every few

minutes when someone needs something." I gave him a half-smile. "What's up?"

He sighed, leaning on the bar. His upper arms pushed against the sleeves of his polo shirt, and I swear, *I* wanted to sigh. "I have a problem."

"If she's five-five, blonde, and comes with a side of bitch, I can't help you."

"Not Claudia. Surprisingly." His lips pulled to the side. "My sister."

"Your sister? What does that have to do with me?"

"You know how she emailed you in response to your ad, and that's how you ended up as my date?"

I paused as someone approaching the bar got my attention. "I don't think I like where this is going."

"You probably don't," he admitted. "Go serve your customer before I tell you."

"Great. I'm not scared at all." I did just as he'd said, serving the guy three beers and pocketing the change at his insistence. "Spit it out. Don't beat around the bush."

"Last night, my sister told my parents that we're dating."

I froze.

Head. To. Freaking. Toe.

She did—that we were—what?

"I'm sorry, what?" I reached up and mimed cleaning out my ear. "I don't think I caught that."

"She told my parents we're dating."

"You're right. I don't like where this is going."

"Neither do I, if I'm honest. No offense."

83

"None taken." I folded my arms across my chest. "But you should probably get to explaining."

Mason sighed. "My sister is a pain in my ass. My mom is on my back about dating, and Kirsty told her we're in a relationship. I tried to pass it off as nothing serious, but my mom is like a dog with a bone. She invited you to both my grandpa's birthday on Saturday and his dinner on Thursday."

I blinked at him. This was not happening. There was no way this was going to last beyond that one night. No way. Nuh-uh. It wasn't happening.

"I don't understand what you're getting at here. I agreed to the reunion because I kind of got myself into that situation."

"I know." Mason rubbed the back of his neck with a grimace.

"Mason, if you're suggesting that I actually pretend to be your fake girlfriend for longer than one night, I think you're out of your goddamn mind."

"I tried to get out of this, I swear."

"Then try harder!" My voice was getting shrill. "Oh, my God. This situation is not normal. You have to see that."

"I see it. I do." He held up his hands. "And I know it's insane. You just have to say that you're working all weekend and you can't attend either, then we can quietly break up, and nobody will know any better."

"Oh, is that it?" I folded my arms across my chest. "It was supposed to be one night only! And even then it was a joke!"

"I know. I don't like this, either. Just tell me you're working all weekend and it's a problem solved."

I pressed my lips together. "I can't do that."

"Why not?"

"Because I'm not scheduled to work this weekend."

"Are you kidding?"

"Hey, you're the one who walked into here and threw this shit out at me. I'm sorry my schedule doesn't line up with the acting career you want me to take up."

He sighed, pressing his fingers against his temples. "You're off all weekend?"

"Yep. I finish at five on Friday, and that's it until Monday lunchtime. My boss is training a new girl, so I got time off because I've worked a lot."

"Fuck me dead."

That wouldn't be so bad…

I darted away to serve a group of customers before coming back. "Look, Mason, we don't know each other."

"I know."

"This is insanity. You have to see that." I flattened my hands on the bar and leaned forward. "It was one thing for one night, for like an hour, to get under the skin of your ex-girlfriend. You're essentially asking me to be your girlfriend for a weekend to impress your mother."

He grimaced. "It does sound insane when you lay it out like that."

"Really? It didn't sound insane before?"

"Yeah." He rubbed his hand down his mouth, hiding a smile. Then, he laughed. "Come on. It's crazy. I don't like this either, but I don't think I can get out of this. She's pretty adamant that you come to one or the other."

"And you can't tell your mom no?"

"You haven't met my mom."

"If you can't tell, I'm trying to keep it that way."

Mason buried his face in his hands and laughed. "It'll be fun?"

I raised my eyebrows. "You don't sound so sure about that. Do you need a minute to decide?"

"I need a minute to think about why I'm here, talking to you," he replied dryly. "Has anyone ever told you that you're hard work?"

"On a daily basis," I said brightly. "That's why I'm single. Nobody wants to come home from work and have to deal with another full-time job in the shape of me."

He glanced down my body. "Then you've got the perfect excuse for us to break up. Come with me, pretend to date me, and be a diva."

I flicked my attention to the person waiting for me to serve them. "Yeah, right. I've met your ex. You could take a cockroach as your date, and they'd accept it as an upgrade."

He laughed into his hand as I skirted up the bar to serve the guy waiting. He took his tray of G&Ts back to his table, leaving me to go back to Mason once again.

What he was proposing was completely and utterly ridiculous. There was no way I was going to do this.

Was there?

No. Why was I even considering it? This was insane. He was insane. Being a pretend date for a stranger for one night was fun, but pretending to be his girlfriend? I got nothing out of this. It wasn't even like I'd gotten myself into this. No, it was his sister. She was the culprit for all of this, and I didn't need to quiz Mason further to know that he wasn't interested in doing this either.

"Why don't you just tell your mom the truth?" I asked, cocking my hip and leaning against the bar, running the cloth between my fingers. "Tell her we went on one date, but your sister lied about the relationship."

"I tried doing that this morning. You have to understand that my sister is her little darling; she can't comprehend a world where she lies."

Ugh. I felt that. "So she misunderstood. There are so many ways you can play this other than having me pretend to be your girlfriend."

"You think I don't know that?" He sank the rest of his beer and slammed the bottle against the bar. "Lauren, I'm stuck between a rock and a hard place. I don't know what to do—my mom is like a dog with a bone when she sinks her teeth into something."

"Mine, too. I get it. But neither of us benefit from this fake relationship." I cupped my hands over my face and groaned.

"I'll buy you a burger. And your drinks. And you absolutely do not have to do anything other than put your arm around me once in a while."

I peered at him and dropped my hands. "I thought you didn't want to do this."

"I don't. But I don't have a choice." He leaned forward and held out his hands. "And we both totally get something out of this. Didn't you say once in a text that your mom and sister are on your back about dating?"

I paused. Iz was more teasing me about being single,

but my mom was one phone call away from setting me up with one of her friend's sons. "Yes," I said slowly.

Mason raised his eyebrows. "Two weeks. We date for two weeks and amicably break up at the end of it. My mom is happy. Your mom is happy. You're happy. I'm happy."

I stared at him for a long moment. There would be worse things in life than actually pretending to be his girlfriend. "Fine. But there are boundaries. This is staying as platonic as possible."

Otherwise, I'd jump his bones. One particular bone, actually…

"I completely agree." He tilted his head to the side after looking at the door where a large group of people had just walked in. "Shall we meet tomorrow for lunch and figure it all out?"

I wrinkled my face up. "I suppose. But you're still paying."

Laughing, Mason stood, leaning over the bar. "I can cope with that." Then, he kissed my cheek.

Blood rushed to my face before he'd even finished pulling away. Despite that, I glared at him and said, "That's a boundary."

He grinned, winked, and turned away, leaving me to burn a hole in his back until I could no longer see him.

♥

"Don't you think it's insane?"

Iz adjusted her shirt so that her nipple was covered and looked up at me. "Yep."

I waited for her to elaborate.

She didn't.

"Just 'yep?' Is that all you have to say?" I stopped my pacing and perched on the arm of the sofa. "Iz, this isn't a fun date. This isn't a one-time thing. This is potentially being his girlfriend for two weeks and meeting his family. There are lines being crossed here!"

She sighed. "Stop shouting. You're making Cara fuss."

I glanced at my snuffling niece. "Sorry."

"Look, you're seeing him soon. Just tell him no, you can't do it. It's not your responsibility to get his family off his back about dating."

"It'll get Mom off of mine if she thinks I'm dating someone."

"She'll plan your wedding if she thinks you're dating someone."

"That's not the point. She might give me a break for a while. It's basically the only good thing I'm going to get out of this."

"So do it."

"I don't know if I want to."

"So don't do it."

"I don't know that I shouldn't."

Iz sighed, shifting slightly and motioning for me to pass her a pillow. I passed her the kidney-bean shaped pillow she used to hold Cara when she was feeding her, and she got comfortable. "What's the worst-case scenario here? Someone finds out? You get real feelings for the guy and decide that you want to actually date him? That you have to hang off the arm of a disgustingly hot guy for two weeks?"

I didn't answer. I guessed it was the second one because Mason was definitely the kind of guy I could catch feelings for if I was given a chance.

The only thing I wanted to catch was a flight to Bali.

"Exactly," Iz carried on. "None of those things are bad. Awkward, embarrassing, mildly uncomfortable? Sure, but that's just an average first date for you."

That was painfully true.

"Ugh. Fine. I'll do it."

"Of course you will. You already told him you would."

"Why do I come here with my issues?"

"Because I'm your worldly big sister who managed to keep a guy so interested that he married me." She grinned. "It means I'm clever and I know things."

"If you say so." I rolled my eyes.

"Laur, listen to me. Just do it. Just have fun. You're single; he's single. It's not gonna hurt either of you to do this dumb thing for two freakin' weeks." She pulled Cara from her boob and, after quickly covering herself up, laid her against her shoulder to burp. "You're going to have fun. You told me that you enjoyed that night with him, and any man who buys you a cheeseburger is a winner in my books."

I pursed my lips. "All right. I'll go and meet him, but there will be rules."

"Smart girl. Set rules. Condoms must be worn before the train can enter the tunnel."

"No."

"Foreplay is a necessity before the bear can enter the cave."

"Please stop."

"Kissing before the submarine enters the sea."

"I'm going to leave now." I stood and grabbed my purse from the armchair. "I'll call you."

"Cakes aren't the only things that need to be moist!"

I slammed the door to her house behind me before I had to hear any more of her terrible, cringe-worthy sexual innuendos.

And absolutely none of those would be mentioned in my conversation with Mason.

CHAPTER NINE

Lauren

"SORRY I'M LATE." Mason slid into the booth opposite me. "I couldn't get away until now."

"It's fine." I smiled at him across the table. He looked unfairly hot to say that he had a big swipe of dirt across his right cheek and dust dotting his hair and his stubble.

Maybe that was why he looked so hot. He already had rugged good looks—he wouldn't be out of place as a lumberjack in a checkered shirt, cutting wood. The dust and dirt on him just…fit.

"Did you order already?" He grabbed the menu from the holder and scanned it.

"No, I waited for you." I smiled. "Busy day?"

"If only roofs built themselves." He returned the smile. "Are you ready to order?"

I nodded, and he flagged down a server. I ordered the hot dog and he ordered the wings—color me surprised—and she wrote that down with a promise to return quickly with our drinks.

"Shall we cut to the chase, then?" I didn't want to be here any longer than necessary.

"Let's." He smirked.

I ignored it. "If we're going to do this, there really does have to be ground rules. It's not going to be easy to pretend we're actually seeing each other."

"We did a pretty good job last week."

"For an hour, Mason. Besides, that was to spite your ex, not convince your mother I'm falling in love with you."

"Point taken." He paused as my shake and his coffee were laid on the table. When the server left, he continued, "How do we start with this? Do you have a pad and paper to write down the rules?"

"No. I'm not that anal." I rolled my eyes. "But we do need to agree on the boundaries, and I think the first one should be that we don't get physical."

"How physical are we talking?"

"Hand holding and hugging are on the table. Everything else is off."

His dark eyebrows shot up. "That's it? I can't kiss your cheek or the side of your head? I mean, I understand taking blow jobs off the table—I can't say I'm a fan of it—but cheek-kissing? Come on."

"Blow jobs were never on the table," I replied. "In fact, blow jobs are so far under the table it'd make your dick shrivel up if it knew just how far."

"I thought this was a negotiation."

"I'm trying to convince your mother I'm your girlfriend, not your penis."

"Hey, it'd be reciprocated."

"You'd have a hard time giving me a blow job unless you're into some kinky shit."

He leveled me with a hard stare. "You are hard work, Lauren."

"I know." I smiled, tilting my head to the side. "I will negotiate to cheek-kissing and other non-sexual forms of kissing."

"There are non-sexual forms of kissing?"

"Have you ever seen someone kiss someone else's toes? The only toes that should be kissed belong to babies."

"Some people like that."

"Do you find toe-kissing sexy?"

Mason paused. "Can't say I've ever kissed a woman's toes. Here, give me your foot."

I tucked them right under my seat. "You're insane."

"I know." He winked. "Okay, physical affection is non-sexual kissing, hand-holding, and hugging. I think we're agreed there. Are we sticking to the 'met on an app' thing we had before?"

I nodded. "I think we should keep it as simple as possible. It's casual, not serious, and we're still getting to know each other."

"Not a lie," he pointed out.

"The best lies skirt the truth. How long have we been seeing each other?"

"Less than a month."

"Smart. Makes it believable when I play the demon and dump you because your family is full-on."

He waggled a finger at me. "And makes me the demon when you tell your family the same thing."

"Exactly. Now you're getting it." I grinned. "Okay, other important information about each other. What do we need to clear up?"

Our food was brought out just then. We both assured the server that we didn't need anything else and got back to our conversation between mouthfuls of food.

"I don't know. Random facts about each other?" Mason suggested. "Do you have a crazy ex I should watch out for?"

"Nope. I do have a raging asshole of a cat, though. Remember?"

"Yep. I have a raging asshole of an elderly next-door neighbor."

"Thankfully, I don't have one of those."

"Yeah, well, if you ever come to my apartment, don't be offended when she threatens to shoot a 'floozy' for knocking too many times on my door."

I raised my eyebrows. "Do you have many women banging down your door?"

"Two weeks ago, she accused the UPS woman of sleeping with me. So, no, but it doesn't bother her. She still thinks every woman at my door is part of some sort of harem."

"She sounds fun. I'd take her to girls' night."

"You really wouldn't. She didn't believe that my sister

was my sister for a year and a half. I still don't think she entirely believes me now, and she pulled out her fucking passport once."

I laughed, choking on a fry. "Okay, that's a little too crazy, even for my girls' night."

"Does your girls' night get crazy?"

I snorted. "The last one ended with me going on a fake date with you. It's not balls to the wall partying, but it's hardly a snoozefest."

"No wonder my sister picked your ad. She'd fit right in with your friend group if that's the case. Pretends she likes to party, but she'd rather be in bed."

"I feel that in my soul. Being in bed doesn't involve heels."

"Ah, I don't think you're going to bed with the right people."

"I'm going to bed with my cat. As long as I pet him between the ears, he doesn't care what I wear to bed."

Mason laughed and picked up a wing. "What a hot date."

"You have no idea. Henry has it going on." I met his eyes with mine and quickly dropped my gaze so I didn't burst into giggles. "Okay, where do I need to be on Thursday?"

"I'll pick you up," he said, covering his mouth with a napkin. "That way, I know you won't run away halfway through."

"Damn it, it's like you read my mind."

"Call it a sixth sense." He smirked. "My grandpa is kind of ornery, so dinner is early. Can I pick you up at five?"

Damn. That was early. "Sure. Do I need to dress fancy? I'm not sure I can take two fancy nights in one go."

"No. Make sure you wear shoes you can run in, though, just in case we need to make a break for it. All my elderly relatives will be there, and things can get a little…crazy."

"Crazy how?"

"Well, my great-aunt Pru likes cocktails with dirty names," he said slowly. "And my great-uncle Charlie has a book of checks for sexual favors that he carries around with him and hands out to women he thinks are hot."

"Oh. Wow."

"And Grandpa Ernie just thinks he's hot and that every woman wants him. He once tried to do a striptease. At my parents' anniversary party."

"Wow," I repeated. "And that's just the dinner?"

"Sadly. That's just the dinner." Mason paused. "Maybe you should see some family tapes to be adequately prepared for this hellhole I'm dragging you into."

I looked down at my half-eaten hot dog. "I think I'm gonna need a meal a whole lot fancier than a hot dog."

♥

That was how, the next day, Mason Jackson ended up in my apartment between his work shift and mine. He'd come armed with a laptop tucked under his arm and a cheeseburger from my favorite burger bar in town.

What? I wasn't going to be eating dinner because of this. I needed sustenance if I was going to work until midnight.

I still had my doubts about this, but my sister was right—there were worse things I could do than pretend this hunk of hotness was my boyfriend.

Having a fake boyfriend was better than no boyfriend at all, right?

I sat down next to him on the sofa with my burger and wriggled to get comfortable. "All right, let's do this."

"I don't think you're ready for this."

"You're probably right." I picked up the burger and took a big bite. "But let's do it anyway."

Mason side-eyed me. "I think I might know why you're single."

I shrugged, chewing the burger, then swallowed before I spoke. "I don't care. Take me at my burger-eating, hot-dog-loving, full-mouth-speaking self, or get outta here."

He looked at me for a long moment before he chuckled, shaking his head. "You're refreshing, do you know that?"

"Like a box full of ice-pops," I replied. "Now play these videos."

"All right. The first video is from my sister's twenty-first birthday." He double-tapped the trackpad on the laptop and the screen filled with a video. It was of an older woman, dressed in a knee-length, bright red dress and a while shawl. White curls framed her face, and I watched with mild amusement as some country music kicked in and she grabbed a handful of her skirt and kicked up a line dance.

Slowly, a host of other elderly people joined her, and

the music changed to some weird remix of Luke Bryan. None of them missed a beat.

I was impressed.

"See, I can't line dance now," I said, wiping the corner of my mouth to get rid of some wayward ketchup. "So the fact they can do it at, what, eighty? That's impressive."

Mason wrinkled his face up. "You're weird."

"Yes." I drew the word out slowly. "I think that was established with my weirdo ad offering my fake dating services."

"Huh. I didn't think of it like that. Not sure what that says about me."

"That you're a weirdo, too." I got up and grabbed two bottles of water from the fridge. "Is that the worst your elderly relatives did? Because my grandpa took us fishing in Alaska when I was thirteen and I had to watch him roll up his pants, showing his little chicken legs, all because he wanted to show us how he could catch a salmon with his bare hands."

Mason's finger hovered over the trackpad as he looked at me. "Did he catch one?"

"No. It jumped out of the water and smacked him in the face. He doesn't do that anymore."

"Smart man."

"A smarter man would have stuck to a fishing rod. Anyway, what other clips have you got on here?"

"All right, I was going to save this, but since you found the line dancing perfectly acceptable…" He tapped on another video. It burst to life, filling the screen. "That's Grandpa Ernie."

I watched as the old man with a rounded belly and a walking stick started to sway side to side to Ed Sheeran's "Shape of You."

"I don't see the problem."

Mason sat back on the sofa. "Keep watching."

This was a trap, wasn't it?

It felt like a trap.

I watched for a good minute and nothing happened. Just his grandpa, swaying side-to-side, to Ed Sheeran.

Then, the beat kicked in.

And so did Grandpa Ernie.

His walking stick was discarded with a flourish, and he ran his hands over his body like a drunken stripper before he did, in fact, strip off his shirt.

To reveal a latex shirt.

"Um," I whispered.

Mason muffled a laugh.

Grandpa Ernie moved to unbutton his shorts while a group of older ladies hollered and whooped like it was a bachelorette party.

"Mason, I'm scared."

"You said you didn't see a problem."

Grandpa Ernie slid down his pants to reveal a pair of leather budgie smugglers.

"There's a problem! There's a problem!" I quickly shut the laptop down and scrambled back on the sofa. "My eyes!"

This time, he didn't hide his laughter. It was so loud

that it attracted the attention of Henry who, sensing new blood, bounded over to the sofa.

I knew what was happening.

I was going to let him do it, too.

Hey—if you show someone a video of an old man stripping to leather sex clothes, you deserve to have a cat sit on your head.

Mason threw his arm over his eyes as he laughed so hard he had to clutch at his stomach with his other hand.

And, Henry being Henry, stopped to look at me with a questioning tilt of his head. When I didn't tell him to stop, he plodded across the back of the cushions and dumped his chubby self right on top of Mason's head.

He stopped, his laugh petering out. "Uh, Lauren? Is your cat sitting on my head?"

"'Row," Henry mewled.

"That's yes in cat," I replied.

"Why is he sitting on my head?"

"Because Henry's an asshole."

Henry responded by licking his paw.

See? Asshole.

"Right. Can you get him off?"

I leaned against the arm and hugged my knee to my chest. "I don't know. You could have warned me about the leather wonder I was about to be exposed to."

"Then you wouldn't have watched it."

"Of course I wouldn't have, you lunatic. I'm going to have nightmares about that for weeks. Did you see that?"

"Yes. I was there."

"Then you deserve my fat cat sitting on your head."

"This is against my human rights."

"Seeing your grandpa in leather budgie smugglers is against mine!"

He fought laughter again. "You're not going to move the cat, are you?"

"Not on your life."

Mason sighed. "Aw, look at us. Our first real fight as a fake couple."

Henry bounced off his head to a sunspot on the windowsill, apparently done with being my revenge plan.

"Yeah, well, I take my apologies in size Sauvignon Blanc."

His blue eyes dragged a path over my body as he looked me up and down. "I've seen you eat nothing but junk. Are you one of those irritating people who can eat what they want and put on no weight?"

"Okay, first." I held up one finger. "You look like you could walk into the cast of the Avengers, so don't come at me with that. Also, I run. Every day. And I don't always eat junk."

"You run?" His eyebrows shot up.

"I don't know if I should be insulted or not."

"No, I just—you don't look like a runner."

"And you don't look like Chris Hemsworth, but here you are on my sofa looking like a dark-haired Norse god," I shot back. "What's your point?"

He held up his hands, fighting another laugh, one that

made his eyes shine. "Hey, I have a physical job. I rarely get to the gym, but I'm always moving."

"Have you ever worked behind a bar? I'm not exactly running a call center back there. It never stops sometimes."

"Do I look like I mix cocktails?"

Doing what he'd done just minutes before, I took a long, hard look at him, from head to toe.

It was a mistake.

If I were a sloth, I wouldn't just climb him like a tree; I'd hang off him for a nap, too.

Lord, he was hot.

Focus, Lauren.

"No," I said. "You look like the lone wolf who waits for the cocktail-drinking girls to accidentally spill their drinks on your shoes." I glanced at the time. "Speaking of, I have to go and make those cocktails."

Mason grinned. "You want me to come and get hit on by drunk girls?"

"As someone who has no say in your life whatsoever, I don't care what you do." I stood up and looked at him over my shoulder. "As your fake girlfriend, I'm a bit of a tiger, so I wouldn't."

"I know." He snorted, following me to the front door with his laptop tucked under his arm. "I've seen you play the possessive girlfriend. If this weren't all fake, I would have been a little turned on."

I locked the front door and tossed my hair over my shoulder. "Please. You were totally turned on."

He said nothing as we headed for the stairs.

"You can say something. That was a joke." I glanced at him, heat rushing to my cheeks.

His lips pulled into a smirk, eyes flashing. "I reserve the right to not respond."

Oh. My. God.

Scratching behind my ear, I dipped my head and almost tripped over my own feet. Mason grabbed my arm, steadying me, then slid his fingers up over my shoulder to tilt my head up with two fingers.

My eyes met his.

"You're cute when you get flustered."

"I am not flustered!"

"Your defiance doesn't make you any less cute. In fact, it's a little hot." He winked, dropping his hand and turning, disappearing down the stairs before I'd even managed to mentally form a sentence together.

"I'm not flustered!" I yelled into the stairwell, chasing him down.

"Still cute!" he hollered back with the sound of a door opening.

I kept running until I reached the lobby. The front door was just about to click shut, but I caught it before it did and stepped out into the late afternoon sun.

Mason was nowhere to be seen.

"Damn it," I muttered, clutching my keys. "Freakin' men."

CHAPTER TEN

Mason

LAUREN: I was not freaking flustered.

LAUREN: Or cute.

LAUREN: The last time I was cute was before I could talk.

LAUREN: And I DON'T GET FLUSTERED, MASON.

LAUREN: Jesus, I hate you.

I laughed and locked my phone. She'd totally been flustered—the bright pink of her cheeks had given that little secret away. There was also a part of me that was regretting the pretending to be in a relationship thing, because if she couldn't pretend not to be flustered…

That was before I even considered the fact that I was looking forward to seeing her again.

That was a real fucking problem.

And I hated myself for it already.

It would be all too easy to pretend to be with Lauren. I didn't have to spend a party with her to know that. It was too easy at my reunion. It was too easy at the bar, and the diner, and at her apartment. Even when her jerk of a cat sat on my head.

And when we'd stopped on her stairs and I'd tilted her face up, it'd taken every bit of self-control I possessed not to kiss her.

To brush my lips over hers, to see if her lips were as soft as they looked.

I rubbed the back of my neck and got rid of those thoughts before they went too far. She'd already made her position clear; anything more intimate that hand-holding and hugging was off-limits, and I was going to respect that.

I wasn't going to force her to do anything she didn't want to do. Except for watch weird videos of my family members.

Hey—she was going to see it in real life. At least now she knew what to expect and she could react appropriately.

Three knocks at my truck window jolted me out of the hole I was thinking myself into.

I pressed the button to lower the window and looked into the scowling face of my great-aunt.

"Are you coming in or what? I'm not paying you to sit in your truck on my drive with a fairy tale look on your face."

"Aunt Pru, you aren't paying me at all."

"I know. But I'm paying you the honor of gracing you with my presence, aren't I?"

"You're right. Forgive me." I hid the twitch of my lips and motioned for her to step back so I could get out. I paused to grab my toolbox from the passenger seat and jumped out after her. "What's the emergency?"

"My new clock needs hanging."

I stopped halfway to the front door. "You called me here immediately after work to hang a clock?"

"Yes. I've been waiting for your father to do it for a week."

"So why didn't you call Dad?"

Evil amusement flashed in her dark-blue eyes. "My panicked calls don't work on him anymore. You're a real sucker."

I took a deep breath and grimaced. She was right. I was. "You win. Show me the clock."

Her cackle wouldn't have been out of place in a Disney movie—with her as the absolute villain. Hell, she'd probably dress as Maleficent one time before she died.

She'd probably make that outfit her funeral one. She'd be buried in it, and she'd go fucking laughing.

I followed her through to the kitchen. The eccentric style of her house barely even registered now. Except for the bright yellow living room curtains and a fox's head on the wall—those were always a little on the jarring side.

The fox's eyes just kind of...watched you.

"Where do you want it, Aunt Pru?"

"Right there." She pointed to the place where her old clock had been. The nail that had previously held it up was still in place.

"The nail's still there. Why do you need me to put another one up?"

"Because that's my clock." She pointed at a huge, iron clock that was twice the size of the last one. "And I don't think the nail is going to hold it."

No. No, a nail was not.

"Jesus, Aunt Pru. You're lucky I brought my drill." The woman was insane. Who needed an iron clock?

Nobody. That was who.

Still, I got to work like she wanted. She fixed me a coffee while I started drilling, and it wasn't until I was done putting the hole in the wall that she finally talked to me again.

"Your mom told me about your new girlfriend."

Of course she did. "Mmm," was all I replied.

"What's she like?"

"She's nice."

"Nice? Screw me sideways, Mason. My tablecloth here is nice. It doesn't sound like you like her that much at all."

She was baiting me. "Mhmm. She's a nice girl. It's early days. Mom's getting a little carried away."

"You know your mother. If she were an ant, she'd be the one carrying food back."

"Probably." I fitted the correct fixture to hold the clock. "You're going to Grandpa's dinner, right?"

"I am. Will I meet her?"

"What do you think?"

"I think you're full of crap."

I turned, raising an eyebrow. "What?"

"It's 'excuse me,' not 'what?' You're not a hooligan." Her eyes sparkled. "Kirsty told me what she did. That girl is a chip off the old block!"

Great. Now my loose-lipped, line-dancing great aunt was in on this thing. "She's a pain in my damn ass," I replied. "She has no idea what she's doing."

"I don't know. It's about time you got back out on the market before you go stale. Women are starting to date younger men, did you know that? I see it all the time on that celebrity channel with the housewives."

I wasn't going to ask what she was doing watching those shows. Probably getting inspiration for her own future toy boy. I wouldn't put anything past her.

"I can't say I follow celebrities much." I turned and leaned against the counter. "I don't know what Kirsty's playing at, but I'm in the shit, especially if Mom falls in love with her. You know what she's like."

Aunt Pru's eyes twinkled. "What if you fall in love with her?"

I gave her a withering look and moved to grab the clock. It was lighter than it looked, and I picked it up easily. "Not going to happen. She's a great girl, but I don't want a relationship right now."

"I think the gentleman doth protest too much."

"Isn't that 'the lady doth protest too much?'"

"Yes, but unless your penis has suddenly shriveled up inside you and you've grown yourself some ovaries, you're not a lady, child."

I was going to take back the times I'd told Lauren she was hard work—she was a delight compared to Pru.

"Whatever you say." I hung the clock on the wall. "Is that straight?"

"Are you straight?"

"What?"

"You don't want a relationship. Did that hooker mess you up so much that you're now gay?"

Jesus. I needed a beer. "I'm straight," I reassured her.

"I'll accept you if you're not, but you're being written out of the will."

"Aunt Pru."

She cackled, rapping her knuckles against the table. "I'm joking. Don't you think I'm funny?"

"My laughter is silent," I said dryly. "Is that all? I can try online dating if I want to be ridiculed."

"Aw, Mason, honey, you have to pay for that. I'm giving it to you for free."

"Well, thank you for the weekly reminder to keep my ego in check." I smirked, putting my drill back into its case. "Shall we do this the same time next week?"

"Yes." She sat back with a smug look. "Bring cookies next time. I need sugar if I'm going to keep this up."

"Noted." I leaned over the table and kissed her cheek. "Don't worry about getting up. I'll see myself out."

"Thank you, dear. Can you pick me up before dinner?"

I paused. "I'm taking Lauren."

Aunt Pru's eyes sparkled. "I know."

I opened my mouth to argue, but she raised her eyebrows, and I knew when I was beaten.

I sighed. "I got you."

♥

MASON: I need to pick you up earlier than planned. My great aunt wants a ride.

I sent the text to Lauren as soon as I got home. I ordered a pizza and took a quick shower before I checked my phone and saw her response.

LAUREN: Is she the line-dancing one?

MASON: Yep. And she knows this isn't real.

LAUREN: …

LAUREN: How?

MASON: My sister is going to kill me one day.

LAUREN: Don't worry. I'll write a eulogy from the perspective of a heartbroken girlfriend for your funeral. I'll wear a face veil and everything.

MASON: Your devotion to me is inspiring. Do you say that to all the guys?

LAUREN: Sure do. It's why I'm single. I say it to scare off the fuckboys. Apparently, it works a little too well.

I laughed as I got up to get my pizza from my front

door. I wasn't surprised at all about that—everything I knew about Lauren screamed that she was the kind of person who got what she wanted in the way she wanted it. Not in a throw-a-tantrum way, but the determined way.

If her first attempt didn't work, she'd think up another way and try again. Rinse and repeat until she got what she wanted.

I admired that.

> MASON: That's one way to narrow the dating pool.
>
> LAUREN: You're the only one who's stuck around, but you kinda have to.
>
> MASON: People always want what they can't have. Want me to flaunt you like girls on Instagram flaunt their asses?
>
> LAUREN: Do you follow lots of those girls?
>
> MASON: No. Sadly, my grandpa does, and he likes to share.
>
> LAUREN: The leather-wearing one?
>
> MASON: Would you be surprised if I said yes?
>
> LAUREN: Absolutely not.
>
> LAUREN: And no flaunting needed. I'm not a surgically enhanced chest.
>
> MASON: I think I'm getting used to your weird comparisons because I didn't even blink twice at that.
>
> LAUREN: It's one of the best things

about me. I'm like a tray of brownies. You don't get to the really good bits until you reach the middle of it.

MASON: What if I prefer the crispy edges?

LAUREN: Then we're a fake match made in heaven. You can have the devil's brownies, and I'll have the soft, gooey ones in the middle.

MASON: Done.

LAUREN: Good. This is going well already. I can't wait for our first real fight.

MASON: We had it already. Yesterday. When your cat sat on my head.

LAUREN: Don't take it personally. Henry sits on everyone's head. It's like his asshole way of showing affection. He's sitting on mine right now.

MASON: It's his way of showing affection?

Her reply was a photo of her and, yep, Henry was sitting on top of her head. He had one paw draped down the side of her face, resting on her cheek, and his tail was curled around her jaw.

She was right. That was an asshole way of showing affection.

MASON: I see. Is that like feline spooning?

LAUREN: I don't know. I wake up with him tucked into my side. It's the only action I get these days.

MASON: Didn't you mention that you're responsible for your own orgasms?

LAUREN: Yes, but I don't do it in front of Henry. Have you ever had a cat watch you while you masturbate?

This was officially the single weirdest conversation I'd ever had with a woman—especially one I wasn't dating and didn't know all that well.

Yet, here we were. Talking about cats and masturbation. Although I suppose I was the idiot who brought it up.

MASON: I can't say I've had the pleasure.

LAUREN: It's the least pleasurable thing you'll ever do. I lock him out now. There's nothing like looking up mid-orgasm and being judged by a cat on top of your dresser.

MASON: So not only does Henry sit on people's heads, he's also a voyeur.

LAUREN: Basically. He's a furry little pervert. Don't show him your grandpa's video, whatever you do.

MASON: There go my plans for tomorrow. I was going to come over and give him a private show.

LAUREN: If you do that and I find cat boy juice in my shoes again, I will rain hell upon your life.

MASON: I'm going to skip over the 'cat boy juice' thing and ask how you're going to rain hell upon my life, because that sounds both terrifying and intriguing.

LAUREN: I'll send you dirty pictures that are both real and fake and you'll have to figure out which ones belong to me and which ones I stole from the internet.

LAUREN: And I'll caption each one with a possessive fake girlfriend line so you get really turned on.

MASON: All I hear from this is that I get dirty pictures of you.

LAUREN: Do you want dirty pictures of me?

MASON: I'm a single, twenty-eight-year-old man who hasn't had sex in months. Let me go ahead and turn you down right now.

LAUREN: I don't appreciate your sarcasm. For that, there will be no dirty pictures.

MASON: Has anyone ever told you that you're ridiculous?

LAUREN: Yes. You. Several times. Are you sure you're not seventy-eight with that memory loss?

MASON: You're feisty tonight.

LAUREN: I'm feisty every night. I

think I was a redhead in another life.

LAUREN: Or an English king. Those guys were feisty AF.

MASON: They also pretty much tried to take over the world in a murderous rage.

LAUREN: Wow. I'm really not as mysterious as I thought. Can't you leave some secrets between us? To keep the magic alive?

MASON: Sorry. I'll pretend I don't know about your secret plans for world domination.

LAUREN: Thank you.

LAUREN: I have to get back to work. Keep that a secret and I'll see that my fleet of white tigers make sure they know you're not dinner.

MASON: You're so generous, Your Majesty.

Her final response was a series of winking emojis with their tongues out, and I burst into laughter. In fact, I'd laughed so fucking hard the entire time I'd basically done an abs workout.

And my pizza was cold.

Goddamn it. The woman was a distraction. A fucking hilarious, beautiful distraction.

I was in so, so much trouble with her. There was no use denying it. She was a little ball of quirkiness in a sarcastic, playful bow. I had no idea where she came up with the shit that came out of her mouth, but I didn't think we'd had a single conversation where she hadn't made me laugh.

I didn't let pizza go cold for just anyone.

I hadn't even realized it was going cold.

I'd just sat down and replied to her, and now, here I was, thirty minutes later, with a cold fucking pizza.

Jesus fucking Christ.

I needed a miracle if I was going to get through this unscathed.

CHAPTER ELEVEN

Lauren

"HELP ME OUT, you jerks!" I shook my phone as if to make my point.

Tina leaned forward on the screen. "Are you wearing your good bra?"

Madi did the same, and I got an unfortunate look up her nostrils. "That's the good bra! I thought you weren't being physical with him?"

I scowled. "I'm not. Can't a girl wear a good bra on a fake date with her fake boyfriend?"

"I don't know. Are there rules on fake boyfriends?"

Tina shrugged. "Never needed to know. Anyone want me to Google?"

"This is ridiculous. Do not Google it." I shook my head and propped my phone up on my dresser so they could still see me, but I had my hands free. "Look. Black dress with the twirly skirt, or the pink dress I wore to his reunion."

Madi wrinkled her face up. "The pink looks great on you, but won't he think you don't have another dress?"

"Do guys even notice that?" Tina asked, cocking her head. "Honestly, when I dated that guy, Keiron, I wore the same dress on our first and third date by accident and he didn't notice."

"That's because it was the blue dress that shows off your boobs," Madi replied. "None of Lauren's dresses show off her boobs."

I scowled. "We're not dissecting my wardrobe and what it does and doesn't show. Which. Dress?"

"Oooh, you're testy tonight. The pink one."

Tina nodded. "I agree. The pink does look really good on you."

I sighed. "I know. But, Teen, the only reason Keiron didn't notice about the dress is because he was a fuckboy. Mason isn't a fuckboy."

"And you base that on, what? One date and a chat in your bar?" Madi asked.

"No. I base it on one date, a chat in my bar, lunch, and an hour at my apartment, plus a bunch of text chats."

"You're spending a lot of time talking for people who are fake dating."

She was not wrong.

We were.

I didn't quite know how I felt about it, to be honest. We had to have a certain ease with each other so that his parents would believe we were actually dating, but it was… too easy.

Like binge-watching an entire season of your favorite show for the fiftieth time.

Easy. Comfortable. Natural.

I was *terrified*.

I was probably the only woman I knew who didn't have a type. Dark hair, light hair, no hair—tall, not so tall, muscular, lean, whatever. All I cared about was that someone could make me laugh.

Anyone who could handle my weird sense of humor and make me laugh was a winner in my book.

AKA, that was Mason.

Which meant Mason was a problem.

A tall, dark, sexy problem.

"Listen, jerks," I said, waggling my finger at my phone camera. "We're not talking about that. He's going to be here any minute, and I don't have anything to wear!"

Tina rolled her eyes. "You have plenty to wear; you're just not wearing it."

Madi nodded. "Go with the pink. It's your color. It's the dress you feel most confident in!"

"And you need to be confident when you meet your fake boyfriend's family, especially since you're crushing hard on him."

"So hard."

"We're done here. You can both fuck off. You're not helping at all." I hung up, but not before the sound of them both laughing filled my room. My phone beeped as the call disconnected, and I groaned, dropping back onto my bed.

This was so fucked up.

So. Fucked. Up.

It didn't matter what I wore. I was going to meet these people twice. None of them cared what I wore. None of them even needed to like me by the end of the weekend.

So why did I care?

Were Tina and Madi right? Was it because I had a crush on Mason?

Oh, my God.

They were.

I did.

I had a crush on Mason.

My cheeks burned, and I clapped my hands over them. Like that would stop it happening. I was mortified at myself and the fact it'd taken me so long to figure that out.

Of course I had a crush on him! He was handsome. I was attracted to him. He made me laugh. And I had to pretend to be his girlfriend… After setting boundaries that he wasn't allowed to kiss me.

Breaking news: Lauren Green was a Class A moron.

Probably not breaking news to my friends who had, apparently, figured this out before me.

How had I not even noticed? Was I so focused on faking everything that I was ignoring my very real vagina tingles toward him?

I was.

I was a terrible excuse for a fake girlfriend.

Sweet baby Jesus, this whole thing was going to Hell in a handbasket, and nobody was navigating it.

Now, I had to pretend like I didn't want to make out

with him like a couple of teenagers.

Great.

There was so much fakery going on even a reality show would be embarrassed to air this.

Oh, come on. Everyone knows reality shows aren't actually real.

Three loud knocks sounded at my front door.

"Shit!" I was still standing in my underwear with my hands on my cheeks. I was officially out of time. Mason was here, and I was panicking in the middle of my room like standing here and doing nothing would solve all my problems.

Spoiler alert, it would not.

Two more knocks.

"Hold on!" I yelled as loud as I could and grabbed the nearest dress to me, which happened to be the pink one.

The one with a zipper on the back.

I didn't have time to tie a string around the zipper to pull it up, so I did the only thing I could do under the circumstances. I yanked the dress up my body, pulled the zip up as far as I could, and ran to the front door, holding the fabric over my bra.

Which I still had to take the straps off.

Oh, my God.

This was a nightmare. I would be mad, but it was entirely of my own making.

Apparently, organization and decision-making were not my strong suits.

I opened the door, clutching tightly at the top of the

dress. "Hi," I said breathlessly.

Mason dropped his eyes to where I was holding my dress. "Problem?"

"Yes. The person who thought of putting a zipper on the back of a dress was either a sadist, a contortionist, or a man."

"Probably a man." He was trying not to laugh as he stepped inside. "Turn around. I'll zip you up."

I blew out a breath and swept my hair to the side so he could. His fingers brushed up my spine as he dragged the zipper pull up to the top, and the warmth of his breath tickled across my shoulder before he stepped away.

"Done," he said in a low voice.

I swallowed. "Thank you."

"You're welcome." It was a little gruff, and he cleared his throat as he stepped back. "Is that the dress you wore to the reunion?"

Pausing, I looked over my shoulder. "Yes. Why?"

He shrugged. "Just wondering. It looks good."

My cheeks flushed. "Thanks. Give me a second, and I'll be ready. Did you already pick up your aunt?"

"No, but she's called five times."

"Am I running that late?"

"No. I'm ten minutes early. She probably wants me to smuggle in tequila so she doesn't have to pay the restaurant prices," he said with a wry smile. "It's why I'm ignoring her."

I laughed and turned. "Give me two minutes. I swear I'm nearly ready."

"Don't rush." He smiled and sat down, leaving me to run into my room and finish getting ready.

I ran the brush through my hair and swept on some pink lipstick before I headed back out into the living room with my purse. "I'm ready."

Mason looked up from where he was petting Henry on the sofa with a smile. "You look beautiful."

Another blush.

Damn it.

"Thank you." I coughed and looked away from him. "Shall we go?"

"Yep." He gave Henry one last scratch under the chin that I caught out of the corner of my eye. "Hey, do you have any tequila?"

I stopped at the front door. "I thought you were trying to ignore your aunt."

"Yeah, because I'm not buying her an entire bottle of tequila. She's already plotting a group line dance for Saturday night. She doesn't need to bring that shit to Thursday night, too. If you have some, I can ration her."

"Are you able to ration her? That was some enthusiastic dancing."

"I probably can't." He sighed. "Never mind. It was worth a try."

"Why don't you call her now to tell her we're coming and can't get tequila but your sister can?"

Mason frowned. "I think Kirsty's already at the restaurant."

I motioned between the two of us. "I think she owes you."

His eyebrows slowly raised as he got what I was saying. "And this is how you'll take over the world, Lauren. Not with a murderous rage, but with cleverly thought-out revenge plots."

I locked the apartment door behind us. "Mostly. Every four weeks I'll change it up to keep people on their toes."

"Why every four weeks?"

I hit the button on the elevator and gave him a sly half-smile. "Because I once read a story where a woman got away with murder by claiming insanity when she was on her period. There's something the English kings didn't have on their side: Shark week."

He didn't say a word until we got into the elevator. "Should I be worried about being in a windowless box with you?"

"Don't flatter yourself. This dress is way too nice to get bloodstains on." I paused. "Probably."

"Hard work," he muttered. "Such hard work."

I grinned.

♥

Pru Jackson's house was the weirdest place I'd ever stepped foot in. Nothing here matched, and the only theme was chaos. A large Persian rug was spread across the wooden floor in the living room. A dark, L-shaped leather sofa took up most of the room, and it was scattered with an array of brightly-colored throw cushions and an afghan that had seen better years, never mind better days.

The walls were a vibrant turquoise that clashed with

the sunny yellow curtains at the windows, and on the wall above the marble fireplace was a stuffed fox's head.

Yep.

Some people had deer horns.

She had a fox's head.

I was beginning to understand the tequila and line-dancing. She was the kind of woman who'd run out of fucks to give by her fifth birthday and couldn't care less what anyone thought about that.

There was a chance we could be friends.

I regularly found myself lacking in fucks.

Unless I stubbed my toe, then they all came pouring out.

"She's very pretty." Pru looked me up and down, her dark blue eyes peeking out from behind bright purple spectacles. "What's she doing pretending to be your girlfriend? She's too pretty to be your fake one, never mind your real one."

Mason took a deep breath. "Ask your great-niece. She's the one who put us both in this situation."

Pru met my gaze. "You couldn't tell him no?"

"He wore me down," I said dryly. "I got the feeling he wasn't going to let it drop."

She nodded begrudgingly. "He does do that. A bit like a teenage boy playing with his tackle. Won't give it up until the cannon shoots. I wish he'd be more like a virgin boy, to be honest. Give up the second the submarine docks in the harbor."

It took everything I had not to laugh. That was the single strangest analogy I'd ever heard for having sex in my life, and my friends were total weirdos.

"We should get going," Mason said, grabbing my shoulders and spinning me toward the front door. "That's enough about me."

"It's never enough about you, boy. I've got a list of grievances, if you'd like to hear them."

"Why don't you keep them up your sleeve for now, Aunt Pru? You never know when you'll need them."

"Quite right, quite right. I've been saving them for my speech at your wedding, but I'm starting to think you'll never get married. Mind you, staying single forever and faking your dates for the rest of your life is better than marrying that other hussy."

Aha. So she didn't like Claudia either. At least I was in good company.

"Mason, why do you have this godawful truck? You know my knees aren't what they used to be."

"Oh, give it up. We've all seen you line dancing, Aunt Pru. Get in the truck."

She huffed but did as she was told, climbing into the backseat with only a little steadying help from Mason. She buckled herself in and leaned forward as he walked to the driver's side. "It's the line dancing," she said conspiratorially. "It makes me feel fifty years younger."

"I've seen a video. I think you're great," I replied.

Mason groaned.

She clipped him around the side of the head. "Let the girl talk. She's smart. I like her. Better than—"

"That other hussy," Mason finished for her. "Yes. Everyone is better than Claudia. If she's the measuring stick for female standards, it's not set very high." He glanced at me before he pulled out. "No offense."

"What if I'm offended?" I replied.

"What?"

"Sounds like you're saying I'm not much higher than Claudia on the standards."

He flicked his gaze toward me. "How do you figure that out?"

"You said no offense. If you didn't mean to offend me, you wouldn't have said it."

He blinked at the road a few times. "I didn't mean to offend you."

"Then why did you say no offense?"

"I didn't—" He paused, flicked the blinker on, and turned. "You're not a low standard. I mean, you're a high—Jesus fucking Christ."

I grinned.

"You did that deliberately."

My grin widened. "You're cute when you're flustered."

His nostrils flared while Pru cackled in the back seat. "I'm not flustered."

"You're so flustered," I retorted. "And cute. So, so, cute."

"All right. I get it. You've made your point." His lips twitched. "No more cute."

I hid my laugh behind my hand. His great-aunt did no such thing, and she laughed the entire way to the restaurant. She only stopped when Mason pulled into an empty parking space.

Then, she leaned forward and tapped his shoulder. "Mason."

"Yes, Aunt Pru?"

"Marry this one. I like her."

Mason's gaze flicked my way. "We're not getting married."

"What's wrong with marrying me?" I asked.

He opened his mouth to speak, then stopped and shook his head. "Nope. I'm not getting into that again. This is a trap."

Laughing, I undid my belt and got out of the truck.

"Seriously," Pru said as Mason helped her out. "Marry her. She's brilliant. It doesn't matter if you don't love her. Hundreds of people marry each other when they don't love each other."

"Yes, but we're not royalty looking to strengthen alliances," Mason replied, locking the truck and offering her his arm.

"Oh, so you're going to let your girlfriend walk in there by herself? Your mother will have a fit."

I understood why Mason could deal with my sense of humor.

"Mom will have a fit no matter what I do. If I walk in with Lauren, she'll complain I didn't walk you in. If I walk you in, she'll complain I didn't walk Lauren in." He rubbed his hand down his face. "Where's the stomach flu when you need it?"

I laughed and took Pru's hand, positioning it inside my elbow. "There. Problem solved. Now be a good boy and hold the door for us."

"Be a good boy?" He stared at me. "I've bitten off more than I can chew. All that can save me now is food poisoning." He crossed his fingers and looked to the sky. "Come on, food poisoning."

Pru chuckled. "I'm having the best time, and I haven't even had a margarita yet! Ay-yai-yai!"

CHAPTER TWELVE

Lauren

FOR THE MOST PART, my introductions to Mason's family were painless. His great-uncle Charlie had tried to offer me a coupon for a striptease which I politely rejected before Mason had thankfully taken me to our seats at the other end of the table.

Which were, unfortunately, next to his mom, Nadia; his dad, Graham; and sister, Kirsty.

It was the height of awkward. His sister kept sending little smirks our way—ones his parents were completely oblivious to. In fact, his mom was nothing but completely sweet, and his dad was genuinely interested in my life.

I felt awful. I was straight-up lying to these people, and it was all because of the other young woman at this table who I knew nothing about. I knew she'd responded to my ad because she hated Mason's ex, but there was no reason for her to drop us in this.

"So, Lauren, you work at The Beachside?" Mason's dad buttered a slice of bread.

"Yes, sir," I replied. "I've worked there for around three years now."

He nodded. "I know Pete. Good man. How do you like it?"

"It's great." I smiled. "Not my first career choice, but I could do worse."

"Oh? What's your first?"

"I'm actually a qualified hair stylist."

"You are?" Mason looked at me. "I didn't know that."

"You didn't know?" His mom raised an eyebrow.

"Uh…"

"The butthead probably never asked," Pru chimed in.

I nodded. "You never asked." *Thank you, Pru.*

"Makes sense." His mom reached for her glass of wine. "You really should ask these things, Mason."

"Noted, Mom, thank you," he replied dryly.

His dad hid a smile. "Interesting. Why don't you work in a salon? If you don't mind me asking."

"A chair rarely opens up in town," I said honestly. "I don't feel like traveling to a salon when Pete is a fair boss. I keep my license valid and do my friends' hair to keep practice up."

"Smart."

I didn't know what to say to that, so I said nothing. Silence hung in the air for a second before Kirsty wiped the corner of her mouth and said, "So, how did you two meet?"

The question was directed at me and Mason, and if I didn't know better, I'd say there was a challenge in her eyes.

We had the attention of the entire table.

Mason slung his arm over the back of my chair as if it was the most natural thing in the world. "Online, actually."

I smiled at him.

"Really?" his grandpa asked. "Are there women wanting some of this online?" When he said 'this,' he motioned his hand down his body.

"I can't say they were in my prospective dates," Mason drawled, looking right at his sister. "Why don't you ask Kirsty? She is online dating right now."

"You are?" His mom's head moved so fast I thought she'd give herself whiplash.

"I'm dabbling," she replied hesitantly. "Why don't you ask Lauren? She was online, after all."

Seriously. Had I once stolen her boyfriend without knowing it or something? What did she have against me?

Instead of glaring daggers at her like I wanted to, I smiled at Grandpa Ernie and said, "Mr. Jackson, I'm sure there are women out there who would be honored to go on a date with you. You should get online and find them yourself."

"A diplomat. They have those in Congress, you know. They're usually known as bullshitters," Great Uncle Charlie said musingly. "Not that I'm saying you are, dear."

"Charles!" Pru leaned across the table and whipped him with her napkin. "Don't be a rude old dolt!"

"Graham," Nadia breathed, pinching the bridge of her

nose.

"Excuse me," I said before it descended in chaos. "I need to use the restroom."

What I actually needed was a break from Kirsty's probing gaze before she said something else that would drop either one of us in it. We were only ready for so many questions, and I had a feeling that she had a list of them, and none of our answers would be correct.

I pushed into one of the stalls and locked the door, taking a moment to breathe. Cupping my nose and mouth, I took some deep breaths. I could do this. We were already halfway through. The pensioners had taken up most of the conversation with their endless—yet amusing—bickering, and it'd only recently turned onto me.

After a couple of minutes, I undid the lock and froze.

Kirsty was waiting in front of the sink area for me. "They're pretty crazy, huh?"

"Yeah," I said slowly. "They are. Excuse me."

She stepped to the side so I could wash my hands. "I feel like we've gotten off on the wrong foot."

"I didn't think we'd gotten off any foot, if I'm honest. I'm pretty much on my ass here."

She grimaced. "You're right. I'm sorry."

"I just—" I stopped and turned, taking a paper towel. "Without sounding like a bitch, what were you thinking?"

Sighing, she leaned against the counter, pushing her dark hair from her face. "Honestly, it was a joke. I never thought you'd agree to it again."

I smirked. "I'm the youngest sister, too. Try again."

"Okay." She laughed, holding up her hands. "I was

meddling. Mase has been single ever since Claudia, and I thought it was time he moved on. You two seemed to have fun at the reunion so I thought I'd try my luck. That's all."

At least she was honest about it.

"Do you know how uncomfortable this is for us?" I asked gently. "Or what an awkward position it puts us in?"

"It doesn't look awkward."

"That's called lying. I'm pretty good at it."

Her lips tugged to the side the same way Mason's did when he was amused. "I'm pretty sure he's feeling something for you for real."

I grabbed another paper towel to finish drying my hands. "It's fine, Kirsty. You know this isn't real, don't you? Don't project something that is—"

The door swung open, and we both froze. Turning, we saw Nadia as she strolled in in her heels.

"Oh, goodness. Are you hiding out in here, too?" She slipped in between us and checked her reflection in the mirror. God only knew why. The woman was flawless.

"Just washing our hands, Mom."

"I don't blame you if you are. Pru just ordered tequila shots." She wiped under her eyes and straightened, smiling at us. "Getting to know each other, are we? What are we talking about?"

I shot Kirsty a panicked look.

"Claudia," she said quickly. "Mom, did you know Mason took Lauren to his reunion last week?"

"Oh, yes. I think you mentioned it." She paused and looked at me. "So you met Claudia."

Her distaste was evident in the bitterness that hardened her tone.

"Unfortunately," I said honestly. "It wasn't the best part of my week."

"Mm." Nadia pulled some lipstick from her purse and slicked it over her lips. "She's not exactly everyone's best friend, is she? Did she act how I assumed she would? Trying to get under Mason's skin?"

"And everyone else's," Kirsty muttered.

I hid a smile. "Pretty much."

"I heard a rumor that a little birdie shut her down."

I glanced at Kirsty. What was she doing? Stop talking. I didn't need Nadia to like me.

She turned to me anyway. "Didn't you basically tell her where to go?" Kirsty continued. "Trevor told me it was apparently hilarious."

"I, uh…"

"Good." Nadia was matter-of-fact. "It's about time someone put that madam in her place." She blotted her lipstick on a paper towel and tossed it in the trash. With one last glance at her reflection, she met my eyes and said, "I didn't think Mason would date anyone worth bringing home if his past is anything to go by. I have to say, I'm more than a little pleasantly surprised by you, Lauren."

Abort. Abort. Abort.

I opened my mouth to say something—anything! Fucking anything!—but I was saved because the door opened again, and Pru burst in.

"Shots for everyone!"

Tequila is never a good idea.

That was why I felt like a giggling little girl. I rarely drank hard liquor, so when I did, it hit me hard.

I'd had three shots.

Three. Shots.

And here Mason was, laughing as I unlocked my apartment door.

"Shut up," I muttered, pushing it open. "Pru is a liability."

"Yes," he said slowly. "But the good news, you totally bonded with my mom over tequila shots and bitching about my ex."

"The way all good fake girlfriends should bond with their fake future mother-in-law. Don't you know anything?" I waved him in. "If I drink coffee now, will I be awake all night?"

"I don't know. Are you a person who needs caffeine to function on a morning?"

"Water it is." I tossed my keys and clutch onto the island and headed for the fridge. "You want one?"

He hesitated.

"I'm not so drunk I'm going to try to jump your bones, don't worry." I pulled out two bottles and pushed one across the island to him.

Well, I tried.

It fell over and mostly…rolled.

"I think that bottle needs to lay off the liquor," I whispered loudly.

Mason laughed and shut the front door. "I think I need to make sure you don't do that on the way to bed."

"Pish. I'm not that drunk. I'm just a little on the tipside of tipsy."

He took the water with a smirk. "I tried to warn you about my family."

"I tried to say no," I reminded him. "You're the one who talked me into this nonsense."

"Ah, but you had such fun."

I stared flatly at him. "Don't push it."

"There's the Lauren I know. Am I getting fed to your white tigers now?"

"You might have too much muscle on you. They might prefer Dr. Evil over a cut-price Thor."

"A cut-price Thor. You wound me."

"Not as much as my tigers will."

"You're pretty confident in your ability to take over the world for a girl who's the worse side of tipsy after three tequila shots."

I pulled a stool under me and sat back, almost missing it before I quickly righted myself. "Look, mister. The best plans are made while under the influence."

"Didn't you put your ad online while drunk?"

"I think you should go now."

He burst out laughing, a sound that warmed my belly in ways it shouldn't have.

No. Bad Lauren. I had no business crushing on this

man. That was my boundary, the line that'd been drawn between us.

No intimacy.

No real feelings.

No relationships.

Neither of us wanted that. I needed to remind myself of those things.

Mason Jackson wasn't the kind of itch you scratched only once; he was the itch that kept coming back in the place you couldn't reach.

The last thing I needed was for that itch to embed itself into my heart.

Wow. The tequila really was doing a number on me.

I turned and opened the drawer, pulling out the bottle of aspirin. I tapped out two pills and tossed them back, swallowing them down with the water.

That was how I knew I wasn't totally drunk. I'd thank myself for this tomorrow.

"You've gone quiet. Are you thinking?"

I looked back at Mason. "Sorry. I thought I'd won that one."

He smirked. "You wish."

"Did you reply?"

"If you didn't hear me, I'm not saying it again." He shrugged a shoulder.

"So no," I said simply. "And yes, I thought I'd thank myself for that aspirin tomorrow."

"Your mind must be a wonderful place."

"You have no idea." I grinned. "So, what are the plans for Saturday?"

Mason's eyebrows shot up. "You still want to go?"

"I don't think I have a choice, but it's nice of you to offer one anyway."

"The party starts at eight. They're old, you know."

"Right. I think I can manage that. Weekend off and all that."

"I forgot." He paused. "You sure you're good to walk yourself down that hall?"

I gave him a withering look. "Yes. I can manage, thank you, Prince Charming."

He held his hands up. "Just checking."

"Your chivalry is noted and appreciated. You'll do well as the head of my knights."

"Now I'm the head of your knights?"

"I'm still figuring it out. How are you with swinging long, deadly weapons around?"

Mason said nothing. His tongue darted out and wet his bottom lip, but there was a flash of laughter in his eyes.

"Um." My cheeks burned. "I didn't mean—I meant a sword. Maybe a lightsaber if I can convince Yoda to share the force."

Still silence.

"Yep, you really should go now." I got up and practically ran to the door.

Mason turned and left his half-finished water on the island. His strides to me were long and purposeful, and he stopped when he was in the doorway. Spinning to me, he said, "I don't think Yoda controls the force, but I'm not really up on Star Wars."

"Me either." My mouth was dry.

He was standing right in front of me. Everything I'd missed earlier tonight was now super in focus for me. From the blueness of his eyes to the fullness of his lips that were surrounded by super-spiky stubbles of beard; the white shirt that hugged every goddamn builder-built muscle of his upper body.

I dropped my gaze for a second. "The last one I watched was the one with Jar Jar Binks. My dad bought me this little rubber Jar Jar whose tongue stuck out when you threw him at the wall and he just kind of hung there. One day his tongue broke, and I was devastated. But I had a Jar Jar toothbrush and everything. I really loved him. Not really sure why."

"What?"

"Oh." I focused on him and saw that he was looking at me with a mix of attraction and something darker—something that held a hint of sexiness. "It's not important. I'm rambling."

"Right." He rubbed the back of his neck. "Sorry. I should get going."

"Sure. Of course. You have to work tomorrow." I gripped the door handle and leaned against the door. "Tonight was fun… In a weird kind of way."

"See if you feel that way tomorrow when the hangover's kicked in."

"I won't be hungover from three tequila shots." I snorted. "I'll sleep in a little late at most."

"Right. Well, you text me in the morning and see how

that's working out for you."

"I'll make sure I do."

"Good." His lips curved up in an unfairly sexy way. "So…goodnight."

"Night."

What did I do now? Shut the door? Kiss his cheek? Wave? What was the polite thing to do?

Good Lord, someone needed to write an article for Cosmo on fake relationship etiquette.

Mason leaned down at the same time I leaned up. I aimed for his cheek but—

Well.

I missed.

A lot.

Instead of hitting the rough stubble of his left cheek, my lips brushed against his full, soft ones. Neither of us moved for what felt like for-freaking-ever—we just stood there, lips together, not touching anywhere else other than there.

It was simultaneously the most awkward and best kiss I'd ever had. It was so painfully innocent, yet at the same time, tingles cascaded over my entire body, from the base of my neck and down my spine, over my arms and to the tips of my fingers where I was gripping the door.

Gripping the door.

Mason was leaving.

And now my lips were on his.

This had gone terribly, terribly wrong.

I yanked myself back, drew in a sharp breath, and

shoved at his chest. He stumbled backward just enough for me to slam my front door and flatten my back against it.

Oh, my God.

My heart was beating like mad, thundering against my ribs, and my entire body was tingling. Tequila and kissing was a dangerously heady mix, and I was right in the middle of that high right now.

Except the high was mixed with the complete and utter embarrassment of accidentally kissing someone you swore you wouldn't kiss—and by total accident.

"Lauren?" Mason said from the other side of the door.

I squealed. "What?"

"I left my phone in your kitchen."

Shit.

I pulled the door open, keeping myself flat against it and, incidentally, hidden behind it.

"Got it." His footsteps paused. "You want me to just walk out so you can slam the door again and pretend that just didn't happen?"

"Yep."

"You got it." A few more seconds and then he said, "I'm outside. Go ahead."

I ran backward until the door clicked shut. "Thank you!"

"Night, Lauren."

"Night, Mason." I locked the door before he could come in again and, after grabbing another water and my phone, ran to my room where I could put yet another barrier between us in the shape of my bedroom door.

It didn't matter that he was probably downstairs and out of the building, meaning he was nowhere near me right now.

I couldn't believe that had happened. That we'd accidentally kissed.

This was why cheek-kissing was bad.

It could go really, really wrong.

And now it had.

Because even as I stripped to my underwear and climbed into bed, pressing the covers against my mouth, all I could feel was the warmth of Mason's lips against mine.

CHAPTER THIRTEEN
Mason

FEW THINGS RATTLED me and got under my skin.

Blood? Not at all. Gore? Not really. Women crying? That I struggled with, but I could cope. A little. I'd survived my sister going through puberty, after all.

Accidentally kissing Lauren Green?

That rattled me.

It was fucking terrifying to think that was the truth. To think that this woman was getting under my skin.

The thought that I was so shaken by a simple brush of her lips, an accidental touch, one that meant nothing at all, had me driven to distraction.

I didn't know what bothered me more: the fact that we'd kissed or the fact that it hadn't been enough for me.

Because it hadn't. It simply fucking hadn't. That one tiny touch had consumed me; it was making me obsess over and over what it'd be like to cup her neck with my hands and kiss her until she melted against me.

Knowing that I couldn't do just that made it worse. It made me want to kiss her more. Out of nowhere. Accidentally. Mid-laugh. Mid-sentence. The first time I saw her. Just before goodbye.

Any one of those situations would work, but I couldn't.

It was off-limits.

Intimacy was. She'd made it clear. I'd agreed. I respected her wishes on that, and I figured she was probably mortified at the fact she'd accidentally kissed me.

She blushed at the slightest thing as it was—something like last night probably had her cheeks on fire all damn night.

The thought of that made me snort. I didn't care what she said. She looked fucking adorable when she blushed, and I wouldn't change my mind no matter how many times she argued with me.

There wasn't long left of this charade. After the party tomorrow night, we only had two or three weeks left, and we didn't even really have to see each other.

It wouldn't be hard to get through. All we had to do was keep our distance. I had a feeling that would be a lot harder for me than it was for Lauren. She was controlled, and I… was not.

At all.

I was definitely more of an impulsive person, which made it all the more impressive that I hadn't grabbed her and kissed the fuck out of her last night. That was what I really wanted to do, and it was a damn good thing that we had today to not see each other at all.

My phone buzzed in my pocket. I put down the sandwich I was halfway through unwrapping and pulled it out, brushing dust from my jeans.

LAUREN: So… About last night.

I grinned. I should have figured this would come sooner rather than later.

MASON: What about it?

Her response was immediate.

LAUREN: It never happened.

MASON: What never happened?

LAUREN: You know.

MASON: I definitely don't.

LAUREN: Don't fuck with me, Mason.

MASON: I'm not. I don't know what you're talking about.

LAUREN: The kiss, jerkface.

I shook my head. She was usually as sharp as a knife, but fuck me dead, sometimes she wasn't all there.

MASON: I know what you're talking about.

LAUREN: Then why would you say you didn't?!?!?!

MASON: You said it never happened. I was playing along.

LAUREN: Oh.

LAUREN: Well, this is awkward.

MASON: Not as awkward as what didn't

happen last night.

LAUREN: True. Look, it was an accident. I went for your cheek.

MASON: I know. Don't sweat it. I'm not going to jump your bones because we both went for the cheek, Lauren. I'm capable of controlling myself.

LAUREN: I never said you weren't.

MASON: If I weren't able to control myself, I'd have fucked you ten times already.

I tore a bite from my sandwich with a grin as time ticked by without a response from her. I couldn't touch her, sure, but it didn't mean I couldn't screw with her a little. In fact, messing with her was becoming a favorite hobby of mine. One I'd miss when this little charade was all said and done.

She was the easiest person to wind up—it was like hitting a light switch and boom, she was riled. And when she got like that, her eyes shone, and she turned into a little spitfire.

Fuck.

I had to stop thinking like that.

How had I gone from being vehemently against a relationship to this? To thinking about Lauren this way?

Thankfully, my phone buzzed again, which meant I didn't have to think anymore about it.

LAUREN: Is that really appropriate here? If you're trying to rile me, it's not working. All you're doing is making this more awkward than it needs to be.

MASON: You sound riled to me.

LAUREN: I'll rile my foot into your balls.

MASON: Feisty.

LAUREN: You're insufferable. Don't you have anything better to do?

MASON: No. I'm on my lunch break. Don't you? Or are you binge-watching on Netflix again?

LAUREN: I don't have to explain myself to you.

MASON: You're binge-watching Netflix.

LAUREN: I was. But Henry's sitting on my head and I can't get the remote.

MASON: You really need to do something about that cat.

LAUREN: Absolutely not. He's a great judge of character. The head-sitting is a thing.

MASON: What does it mean?

LAUREN: That he's an unruly little fucking asshole.

MASON: How does that play into him being a great judge of character?

LAUREN: Omg can you stop dissecting

everything I say? You're a builder, not a psychologist. Go and fix it, Bob.

MASON: Did you just use a Bob the Builder reference on me?

LAUREN: Depends if you can fix it or not. Does your digger talk like Bob's?

MASON: I can't talk to you when you're like this. It's impossible.

LAUREN: That is the word on the street. For a difficult and impossible conversation, call Lauren Green.

MASON: I'll be sure to write that on the wall of the next public bathroom I use.

LAUREN: Don't forget my phone number.

MASON: It's already on the internet.

LAUREN: I need a new number.

MASON: Good. Get one in two weeks. That's how we break up. You get a new number and ghost me.

LAUREN: Done. Now go and build a wall or whatever it is you're doing. I have to shower and go to work.

MASON: How are you gonna do that with Henry on your head?

LAUREN: He's a cat. Say the word 'shower,' and it puts the fear of

God in him.

MASON: True enough.

MASON: I have to get back to work. I'll pick you up at six tomorrow. We've been roped into helping decorate the party room.

LAUREN: As long as your uncle Charlie doesn't offer me another checkbook full of sexual favors, I'll do it.

MASON: Cannot guarantee, but Mom insisted, so sucks to be you.

LAUREN: Yeah, but as my fake boyfriend, you get my complaining. Sucks to be YOU, actually.

MASON: I didn't think this through.

LAUREN: :D :D :D :D :D

♥

I tugged on the collar of my shirt. The pristine white collar was stiff and uncomfortable, and there was no way I was going to last all night wearing this.

This was why I didn't wear the clothing my mother sent. Why I'd even thought this was a good idea was beyond me. There was no chance in hell I was going to keep this on a second longer than necessary.

More to the point: I was twenty-eight. Why the fuck was my mother sending me shirts?

I unbuttoned the shirt and tossed it over the back of the

armchair. Two knocks at my door made me pause. I needed a shirt, but if my neighbor heard that knocking…

"Two seconds!" I called, running for my bedroom.

I pulled a white, short-sleeved shirt from my closet and shrugged it on, masterfully managing to button it halfway before I tugged the door open.

"What the fuck are you doing here?"

Claudia shuffled from one side to the other, pushing her blonde hair behind her ear. "Can we talk?"

"No," I said firmly. "I'm on my way out."

"Please, Mason?" She wrapped some of her hair around her finger. "Just five minutes."

The lock clicked from across the hall, and I did the only thing I could—I let her in. "Five minutes. I have plans tonight."

"With your new girlfriend?"

"What I do is none of your business. What do you want?"

"I want to talk to you."

I buttoned the rest of my shirt and tucked it into my pants. "Talk, then."

"I messed up," she said in a small voice. "I never should have cheated on you."

I stared at her flatly. "Try again."

"Mason, please!" She stepped forward, reaching for me, but I moved back out of her grasp. "You can't tell me that woman is more important to you than I am."

"By that woman, I assume you mean Lauren."

"Whatever her name is. Yes." She moved toward

me again. "Six years, Mason. That's something to think about."

I put my wallet and phone in my pockets and grabbed my keys from the coffee table. "You're right, Claudia. It is. Six years is a long time to be with someone, but you should have thought about the sanctity of our relationship before you decided to wrap your legs around someone else's body because they had more money than I do."

"Mason, it wasn't—"

"We're done here." I opened the door. "I have to pick up Lauren, and I have no desire to hear any more of your excuses. You're only here because I've moved on."

Claudia hauled the strap of her purse up onto her shoulder and pouted at me. "We're not done here, Mason."

"We were done when you shoved your boss' dick down your throat. Out."

She did as I'd said, shooting me one dark look as she disappeared out into the hallway and toward the elevator. The doors opened for her to step inside right as the door opposite me swung open.

Mrs. Allerton hobbled out, staring down the hall after Claudia. "What did that hussy want?"

Usually, I'd correct her, but… "She was trying to get me back, Mrs. Allerton."

"Did you take her back?"

"No, ma'am. I kicked her out."

She grunted. "Good. Can I give you some advice?"

"I'd love it," I said politely. She was going to give it anyway.

"You wouldn't buy a rotten vegetable. Don't date one,

either, especially if you've already thrown it out already."

How about that? That *was* some good advice.

"Solid advice, Mrs. Allerton. Thank you." I stepped out and locked the door. "Thankfully, that ship has sailed and sunk."

She tapped her chin. "She was here the other day. Shall I shoot her if she comes back?"

"Probably best you don't. The building manager doesn't know about your new gun, does he?"

"Hmm. He doesn't." She sighed. "Stupid people. Stupid rules."

I nodded along as if I agreed. It really was the easiest option, and my mind was already whirring with the presence of Claudia.

"Are you off somewhere nice?"

"My grandpa's birthday party," I said. "And I really have to be going before I'm late." I checked my watch. "Thanks for the advice, Mrs. Allerton. I'll keep it in mind."

"You do that, Mason." She disappeared into her apartment and shut the door before I could say anything else or even say goodbye.

Typical.

I shrugged it off and after checking that my door was locked, headed for the stairs. I was hyper-alert as I walked into the parking lot—I didn't want to be blindsided by my ex-girlfriend and whatever bullshit story she wanted to spin me again.

Thankfully, there was no sign of her car or of her, so I climbed into my truck and hightailed it out of there.

Just in case.

I had little time to think about her or her reasoning for suddenly appearing at my front door. The drive to Lauren's apartment was quick and painless, and I shook all thoughts of Claudia away as I entered her building.

I took the elevator up to her floor and stepped out. It was as silent and still as always, and I was starting to wonder if anyone else actually lived in this building. God only knew mine was lively enough.

I was a little jealous of the peace and quiet.

Her door swung open before I had a chance to knock. Lauren looked me up and down with her light-blue eyes, taking every inch of me in. It gave me a chance to do to the same to her.

She'd gone for a black dress today, one that hugged the top half of her body with a neckline that dipped into a deep 'V.' The skirt was full and swayed as she stepped back to judge me. "You're late."

I dragged my gaze up from her chest. Her dark hair was curled and hung over her shoulders, and a light-pink lipstick coated her soft lips.

Shit, I wanted to kiss her.

"Hey!" She snapped her fingers, pulling my attention from her mouth to her eyes. "I'm up here, moron."

"Sorry." *I wasn't.* "Are you ready to go?"

"I just told you that you're late."

"You're feisty today."

"I'm feisty every day. Some days more than others."

"Is this some days?"

"You're standing in front of me, late, and ogling my chest. If it isn't already, it's about to be."

I reached forward and tugged up the neckline of her shirt. "Problem solved."

Lauren leaned forward and covered my eyes with her hand. "No. *That* is problem solved."

"Touché."

She dropped her hand with a roll of her eyes that I only just caught. "Whatever. Let's go before it all goes to shit."

"Before what all goes to shit?"

"The rest of my day." She pushed some hair behind her ear and grabbed her purse. She held the clutch tightly against her side as she all but pushed me out of her apartment and slammed the door shut.

I took a step back from her, keeping my eyes on her as she turned the key with more vigor than I'd ever seen anyone do before. She shoved the key in her purse and slapped the top of the clutch down, then looked up at me.

There was nothing but pure frustration in her eyes.

I did the thing that came most instinctively to me. I reached for her and pulled her against me. She froze, her entire body turning to a plank of wood until she finally relaxed against me. Slowly, she slid her arms around my waist and held me tightly.

It was hard not to focus on how well she fit against me. How perfectly the top of her head tucked under my chin and my hand cupped the back of her neck as I held her tightly.

It was even harder to ignore the way my heart beat a little harder.

Lauren shuddered, her warm breath dancing across my arm when she turned her head. "Thanks. I needed that."

"I could tell." I pulled back, not quite letting go of her, but not quite holding onto her either. "You good now?"

She nodded.

She didn't move away from me, though.

"It's one of those days. My water cut out because the building manager forgot to tell us there was work being done on a pipe and I was halfway through a shower, so I had to wash shampoo out of my hair in the kitchen sink with bottled water. Then Henry left me a present on the windowsill, and my boss called to ask if I could work tonight which I had to say no to because we have these plans, then my sister called and she's having a rough time, so my mom called to tell me I need to support her more because she's not there to do it, and I had to listen to ten minutes of guilt-tripping even though she's on vacation in the Cayman Islands with my dad and their friends."

Wow. She didn't even take a breath through most of that.

"Feel better?"

She blinked at me. "I do, actually. Apparently, I just needed a bit of a bitch."

Grinning, I stepped back, releasing her entirely. "How about we stop and get you a cheeseburger on the way there? That'll cheer you up."

Her eyes lit up. "You're the best fake boyfriend ever."

CHAPTER FOURTEEN

Lauren

"ONE LAP DANCE and I'll never bother you again."

At this point, it was actually a good deal.

I looked at Mason's great-uncle Charlie and shook my head. "I tried to give a lap dance once. I fell face-first into a toilet."

Life lesson learned: don't ever lap dance in a bathroom when the floor is wet. Or when you've been drinking. Or at all.

"All right, how about—"

"How about you leave the poor girl alone, Charles?" Pru swept in with a dry tone and a gin and tonic in her hand. "She doesn't want your sexual favors. She's not going to dance like a puppet for you. Let her drink her wine and judge people with me."

Before he could say a word, Pru grabbed my arm, barely leaving me enough time to pull my clutch against my body and scoop up my wine glass.

Thank God.

I thought I was never getting out of there.

"I wish I could say he was senile," Pru said. "But my brother has always been a dreadful pervert."

Of course. With a personality like that, there was no way it could be anything else.

Pru lead me over to a table that was slightly out of the way and insisted I sit down. I did. I didn't want to upset her—not only was she my only true ally here, but I had no desire to be at the end of her sharp tongue, thank you very much.

"All right, if you're gonna survive this shitshow, here's what you need to know." She put her gin and tonic that, on reflection was probably just gin, down on the table between us. "Avoid Charlie, but you know that already. Alfie, he's the guy in the red fedora, avoid him, too. He likes to pull unsuspecting women into Cha Cha Slide battles."

"Do I want to know what that is?"

"No." Pru sipped her drink. "Now, Elsie is proficient at the Macarena, and while she's fun to drink with, do not let her get you drawn into vodka shots."

I nodded.

"And Shirley—she's the bleach blonde tart with the leopard print shoes talking to Nadia—is a slut for some Fireball. Don't be there when she gets control of the bar. It won't end well for her."

"Right," I said slowly. "So I should hide in the corner

and hope nobody notices me."

"That's about right." Kirsty slid into the chair between us. "What up, Aunt Pru? Pissed anyone off yet?"

"Only your father, but that's par the course." Pru was completely unbothered by it. "What are you doing here? Don't you have a date?"

"I did, but he sent me dick pics, and they weren't that impressive, so I bailed."

"Ah." Pru nodded as if she understood.

Hell, maybe she did.

"How's Mason?" Kirsty nudged my shoulder.

I side-eyed her. "He looks fine to me."

And he did. Fi-*i*-ine. He was at the bar with his buddy, Trevor, who I'd met at the reunion. Apparently, their families were close friends, and that was why he was here tonight.

"Mhmm. Just fine?"

"We've already spoken about this," I reminded her. "I'm here because you made me be. You're responsible for this."

I wasn't in the mood for this tonight. I was here, being nice, being the socially acceptable good girlfriend, despite the bad mood that bubbled underneath it all.

I wasn't over my mom's scolding. She'd gotten under my skin with her hypocritical criticism of me, but that was nothing new. It was the thing I'd grown up with, and Iz had, too, to an extent.

This time, she'd really pissed me off, and I couldn't shake the frustration no matter how hard I tried. After all, I'd been the one who'd been there the day after Imogen had given birth. I'd cooked her meals and bought her beaver-dam-sized sanitary towels. I spoke to her every day, and for my mother to drag me down the way she had really made me mad.

And I hated that Mason hugging me had taken the edge off.

Seriously.

What was he? A human vodka shot?

Now I was here, at his grandpa Eddie's birthday party, with his family, pretending like I was okay, while he stood at the bar with Trevor and watched me with a stupid little smile on his face?

All I could think of was his lips on mine for the few fleeting seconds they'd been there. It was a frustrating balm to my annoyance. The thought of kissing him was way more soothing than it had any right to be.

The idea of Mason running his fingers through my hair while his lips moved across mine, and I ran my hands over his shoulders and arms as our bodies pressed closer together...

Jesus, I was getting a complex with this man.

Complex feelings.

Kirsty grinned. "You're doing a great job at convincing everyone else you're the real thing."

I sipped my wine. "It's not hard. Nobody is paying attention to either of us."

Charlie's attempts at hitting on me didn't count. He'd already moved on to a lady in a fetching violet dress, and I doubted she'd be the last woman in his sights tonight.

"It can't all be fake, though. I mean, he keeps looking

at you."

"Probably to see if you're pissing her off," Pru snapped. "Which you are."

Kirsty looked at me, wide-eyed. "Am I?"

"I wouldn't say that," I said tentatively. What? Fake or not, I wasn't in the habit of being rude to strangers. Unless the stranger was Claudia.

"Oh." Pru finished the rest of her gin. "I guess it's me you're pissing off."

"Let me get you another drink," I said quickly, reaching for her glass. "I'm going anyway." I punctuated that by downing the remaining wine in front of me and getting up so quickly that my head almost spun.

Thankfully, it didn't, and I beelined for Mason and Trevor at the bar.

"What's up?" Mason asked, his eyes never leaving my face.

I set the glasses on the bar with a sigh and leaned forward. "Give your sister a pole, because she's fishing hard."

"What's she fishing for? Compliments? She'll have to try harder." Trevor snorted. "There's nothing to compliment."

I thought Mason would tear him a new one, but he didn't. He simply chuckled his agreement, and I guess he was in the same situation I was: Kirsty deserved it.

"She's fishing for feelings where there aren't any," I said quickly before I grabbed the bartender and ordered new drinks.

Mason rolled his eyes. "I told her to cut that shit out when she tried it with me earlier. Has she forgotten she's the reason we're in this situation?"

"Evidently." My tone was dry. "But feel free to tell her again. She's not listening to me." I passed money across the bar to the tender and handed Mason the gin and tonic. "Take this to Pru before I regret all my life choices even more."

Laughing, he took the glass and left, making his way over to the table where his aunt and sister were sitting.

Trevor sidled up to me. "No feelings, huh?"

I side-eyed him, picking up my glass of wine. "Do I look like the kind of girl who catches feelings like people catch a cold?"

"I'm not gonna answer that. There's no right answer."

"Hey, you're smarter than you look."

"You're witty. No wonder Mason keeps staring at you."

I snorted. "He doesn't keep staring at me."

"Have you been looking at him?"

Yes. "No. He's not a TV."

"Then how do you know he hasn't been looking at you?"

"Because I'm also not a TV," I said dryly. "It's also called a gut feeling. I think I'd know if I was being watched like a cheap studio sitcom."

Trevor blinked at me. "You have one hell of a way with words, Lauren."

I raised my glass to him. "Thank you. I pride myself on it. It keeps people on their toes."

"What does?"

"Never knowing what shit is gonna come out of her

mouth." Mason stepped up next to me and stretched his arm out behind me to grab his beer. "Keeping up with the Kardashians is nothing compared to keeping up with Lauren Green."

"I'm going to take that as a compliment because I'm not sure starting a fake argument here is a good idea." I sipped. "But if you'd like to provide entertainment…"

"Damn, I'm almost hoping Claudia shows up," Trevor said. "I'm still pissed I missed that."

"It wasn't that impressive. Well, maybe to you guys. But for women, it was just a regular way to shut another woman down. We're good at it, given that all women are bitches."

"All women are bitches?"

"Well, yeah. We're all bitches inside. It doesn't matter how hard you try to hide it, it's gonna come out sooner or later. I just prefer to be a bitch to people's faces."

Mason cocked his head to the side. "Why?"

"Because I'm a woman. If I'm a bitch in private, it'll get back to them, and I'll have to be a bitch anyway. I like to cut the middleman and save us all some time."

Trevor choked on his beer. "Seriously, if you aren't gonna date her for real, please let me date her."

"You wouldn't be able to handle me, Trevor. I'd chew you up and spit you out in a night."

Mason nodded. "It's true. She would. She's hard work."

I nudged him. "You're not exactly easy yourself. You are why we're in this situation, if you remember."

"Actually, you are. You're the one who put an ad online."

"Look, if we're going to get into semantics, I can't argue with you, and that doesn't benefit me at all."

He laughed and stepped in closer to me. "Ah, but semantics benefits me. You've shut down the conversation already."

"No, I told you I can't argue with you if you bring semantics into it. I can, however, talk to you and break down all your arguments."

"That's something I'd like to see. Do I have to pay for it, or are the tickets free?"

"You can get a free front row seat since it's you I'm tearing down."

"The romance. I can hardly take it."

"I'll sprinkle rose petals across the floor before I rip your arguments to shreds. How does that sound?"

"If you were a good girlfriend, you'd sprinkle a trail of your clothing toward the bedroom, but whatever."

"Well, thank God I'm not."

Trevor looked between us both with bewilderment in his eyes. "You two need to get married."

With that comment, he left us alone, heading in the direction of where Kirsty and Pru were huddled over the table talking.

"That's two people in your life who think you need to marry me," I said slowly. "Either you need to re-evaluate your taste in women, or I need to stop being so delightful."

"Probably the first one." Mason leaned back against the bar, his finger tickling my arm. "You *are* a real delight, did you know that?"

"I tell myself it every day before I brush my teeth. Putting good thoughts out into the universe and all that."

"I can never tell when you're joking and when you're being serious."

"That's part of the joy of living in my world. Keep up, Mason."

"My bad." He turned his body into me, bringing his mouth to my hair. "My mom is watching us and pointing you out to my uncle. Play along."

I tilted my head as if I was listening to him and moved into him, smiling as I did so.

All right, it wasn't the worst thing in the world.

"How long do we have to keep this up for tonight?" I murmured, lifting my lips close to his chin. "Not that standing next to you is the worst thing I've ever done, but I don't want you getting too attached to me."

Mason chuckled. "Couple hours at least. You agreed to this."

I groaned. "So I did. That was a terrible idea."

"I'm great company."

"I never said you weren't. I'm just not sure I'm that great."

"Well, you're better now than you were. Plying you with wine seems like it's the way forward."

"What are you trying to say?"

"Nothing, nothing." The grin that spread across his face was both playful and sexy. "Don't worry. We'll leave before the old ones get out their cowboy boots and start line dancing."

I wrinkled up my face. "You promise?"

"Promise."

♥

Spoiler alert: Mason Jackson was a big, fat liar.

It was the only explanation for why Pru had wrangled my wine glass out of my hands and guided me into the position I was in now.

In the middle of a line of women who, at a minimum, were old enough to be my mother. I knew only three of the women who were shuffling side-to-side excitedly—Pru, Kirsty, and Nadia.

I'd also seen the videos.

I knew what was about to happen.

I was about to be a line-dancer extraordinaire. I wasn't wearing the shoes for this. Nobody could line dance in four-inch heels. This was going to be a disaster from the very first beat of the music.

"Off." Pru swerved so she was standing in front of me and held out her hands. "Take them off."

I looked at my feet. "No offense, but they're my only line of defense at this point."

"Lauren, remove the shoes, or I'll do it for you."

Shit, she wasn't joking.

I wasn't sure if it was the look in her eye or the four glasses of wine that made me lean on Kirsty's shoulder to stabilize myself while I removed my trusty black heels. Pru took them from me with a triumphant "whoop" and handed them to Mason.

He took them by the heels, looking over at me with confusion glinting in his eyes.

"Help," I mouthed.

He held my gaze for a moment that felt like it lasted forever, then winked. "No," he mouthed right back, using his beer bottle to hide his smile as he wrapped his lips around the rim of it.

Jerk.

I bit the inside of my cheek as the Macarena filled the room.

That's right.

The Maca-freakin'-rena.

No.

This was not happening.

Inside my head, I was at home, eating pizza while Henry sat on my head. In reality, I was stretching my hands in front of me, doing a dance I hadn't done since middle school.

I was doing the Macarena. Barefoot. In the middle of a function room, on the other side of tipsy, with my fake boyfriend's family.

Einstein was wrong. The definition of insanity wasn't doing the same thing over and over again.

This was.

This had to be. It was the only explanation for anything.

Oh, God, what was happening? How had I ended up here? And why the hell was I enjoying it?

We shook and jump-turned for the second time. Kirsty

caught my eye as we laid our arms out in front of us for the third time and winked.

"Welcome to the family." She laughed, knocking her elbow into mine when we both moved to put our hands behind our head.

The only thing I could do was laugh. This situation was insane, and I wasn't quite sure what I was doing here, but I was having fun.

Goddamnit, this was going wrong.

Yet, I still laughed. And when I'd spun enough to meet Mason's gaze again, I caught my tongue between my teeth, grinned, and winked. It was a little saucy, but hey—that was how I felt.

It'd been a long time since I'd let my hair down like this, and after the afternoon of guilt-tripping I'd had, it was worth every second.

Mason hugging me had taken the edge off the tension I'd held in my shoulders but being dragged into dancing with his family had removed whatever was left.

Why were my family parties never this fun?

The Macarena trailed off, only to be replaced with the cheesy, upbeat tune of The Birdie Song.

I looked directly at Mason. He held up his hands, his eyes going wide, and vehemently shook his head. I nodded, and he backed up as much as he could before he hit the bar. Thanks to my lack of heels, I was quick, and I darted across the room to grab him and pull him to the makeshift dancefloor.

"Lauren." He fully groaned my name, but he stopped to put my clutch and shoes on the nearest table.

I put my hands up at my chest and flapped my arms like a bird.

He laughed, throwing his head back at my silliness when I caught my tongue between my teeth and grinned. "You're insane."

"I know." I linked my arm through his, and we spun. "It's another part of my charm."

"Charm. That's one way to put it."

"There's no need to be rude. I've already told you that I'm a delight."

"And I've told you that I agree." He laughed, swinging me around to stand in front of him. "You are a delight."

"It doesn't sound sincere when you say it. Maybe you should wink or give a boob squeeze or something to really drive your point home."

"You want me to squeeze your boob?"

"I didn't say I wanted you to, maybe that you should."

"You're giving me mixed messages here." Mason made the birdie thing with his hands. "Should I squeeze your boob or not?"

"Probably not."

"Agreed."

We linked arms again to dance.

"Don't you want to squeeze my boob?"

"You're so weird." He released me, shaking his head. "One day, you're going to catch me out, and I'm going to be screwed."

I sighed, moving to the side when the song ended. "I know, but I think you're catching on to me."

"Just a little. It's a close one, though." He handed me my glass of wine. "I have to stop and think every single time I reply to you. The whole 'offense' conversation is stuck in my head."

Grinning, I raised my glass to my mouth. "That was fun. But you haven't called me cute since, so that's a win."

"I don't know. Watching you do the birdie dance was pretty cute."

"Wash your mouth out with soap."

"What's your aversion to the word 'cute?'"

"It diminishes things. A baby is cute. A kitten is cute. A dress can be cute. I'm a twenty-five-year-old woman. I'm not small, nor am I an adorable item of clothing that will sit in my closet for six months before I remember I bought it. I'm not cute."

He dropped his gaze to my mouth. "I don't know. This little tantrum is cute, but mostly because you're pouting your lower lip out like I just stole your teddy bear."

I immediately pulled my pout back in and pursed my lips instead. "Shut up."

"Now you're cute because you're sulking."

"You're going to start a fight if you carry on."

"If we fight, we'll have to make up, which means you'll have to kiss me."

I swallowed. "Okay, no fighting."

"Is kissing me that repulsive?"

"No, but it's against the rules."

"There's no need to act like it'd give you nightmares, then."

"How did I act like kissing you would give me nightmares? All I said was that we wouldn't fight. That's hardly me acting like it's repulsive."

Mason shrugged. "I know it's off limits, but would it really be the worst thing in the world?"

"I didn't—I don't—we're not getting into this," I said, shaking my head. I put my shoes on the floor to slip my feet into and paused. "Wait. Did you just do that deliberately?"

Mason frowned. "Do what deliberately?"

"That, just then. Because that's what I do to you."

"I don't know what you're talking about."

"Mason."

"What?" His lips twitched.

"You're trying not to smile at me!" I reached out and slapped his arm. "You did! You did it deliberately!"

He grinned and grabbed my wrist, pulling me into him. "How does that medicine taste, Lauren?"

"Cold. Like my revenge will be." I narrowed my eyes and nudged his chest. "You're a pain in the ass."

"Again… Your own medicine."

I opened my mouth to say something, but Pru appeared out of nowhere and grabbed my hand, pulling me after her before I even had a chance to think.

"Let's go! They're playing sex bomb, and it's stripper time!"

Oh, sweet Jesus.

CHAPTER FIFTEEN

Lauren

"I'M SCARRED, MASON."

He slid the mug of coffee across the island toward me. "Here. Drink this. It'll calm your nerves."

I looked into the steaming mug. "Nothing will calm my nerves. I cannot unsee what I've seen tonight."

Nodding, he let out a long breath as he cradled his own mug. "All I can do is apologize. If I knew it would get that bad, I would have taken you and ran."

"I don't think I can get over this."

"You know you can talk to people about how you're feeling."

"I don't think I can talk about it. It's seared into my brain." I peered over at him. "All I know is I never, ever, ever want a lap dance from an eighty-five-year-old man again."

All he could do was nod his agreement, slowly, and with eyes full of pity. "I have to admit, watching it was painful. I still don't really know how you got wrangled into it."

"It was quite simple. Pru grabbed me, sat me in a chair, and tied me to it with a scarf before I could protest. She's annoyingly quick for an old woman." I shuddered at the memory. "And ties knots better than a pirate. I'm surprised she hasn't taken command of a fleet of pirate ships."

"She tried to. Once. But it was a kid's playground, and they had to call a police officer to remove her." He stirred his coffee and looked up at me with a glint in his eye. "She tells the story differently, but there's no way she's ever wrangled an alligator."

I snorted coffee up my nose. "Ahhh!"

"Sorry." He didn't look sorry at all.

"Whatever." I pinched my nose until it stopped burning. "Is it bad I can imagine her doing that?"

His eyes glittered. "No. But imagining it probably isn't anything nearly as scary as actually witnessing it."

"No shit." I picked up my coffee and made my way over to the sofa.

Mason grabbed his and followed me over, taking the seat next to me. "Sorry you got dragged into the crazy. I actually told them to dial it in a little so they didn't scare you off."

"Scare me off? Are you trying to seduce me into staying?"

"No. But they had to believe I was."

"Wow. No need to shoot me down so brutally."

He rolled his eyes. "Stop it. Don't tell me you're getting sensitive now."

I swallowed, pushing hair from my eyes. "I'm not. I don't get sensitive. I'm not a clitoris."

"You sound sensitive."

"Am I not allowed to be?"

"You just said you don't get sensitive."

"Exactly. I don't get sensitive. Doesn't mean I'm not already."

He looked at me for the longest second, his blue eyes bright yet clouded with questions at the same time. "Are you okay?"

"I'm fine." I smiled tightly and took a big drink of my coffee.

And I was. I was fine. I was okay. I just wasn't comfortable with how I was feeling, which wasn't appropriate at all.

Neither was the lap dance, but I digress.

I was feeling far too many things for the man who was sitting mere feet away from me. There was only so much time you could spend with someone before you really started to feel things for them, and I think we'd crossed the line tonight.

At least I had.

I'd crossed the line. Attraction toward Mason had turned into something a little bit stronger. Real feelings—ones that had the potential to end up with me getting hurt. They were also ones I had to keep to myself, especially now that I was admitting to myself that they existed.

I had feelings for Mason Jackson.

Very real feelings.

There.

The truth was out there.

Well, out inside my head. I wasn't going to say it out loud. That was a recipe for disaster. We'd set boundaries, and I was the one who was overstepping them.

It was what it was. This funk of a mood had come out of nowhere, especially since I had already shaken off one of these today. He'd been the thing to pull me out of the terrible mood I'd found myself in thanks to my mother, and now here I was, back in one, because of myself.

I should have known this would happen the second I answered my door and laid eyes on him.

I should have known I wouldn't be able to keep to any of the rules I'd set. I've been so adamant about sticking to them; repeatedly drawing the line, scribbling over them with Sharpie until I broke holes into the paper.

Now, there was no way I could break them. There was no way I could tell him how I was feeling now.

I finished my coffee and got up, taking the cup into the kitchen. Exhaustion came over me in a wave. Apparently, the wine was more effective than the coffee tonight.

At least I'd sleep.

"Are you sure you're fine?"

I turned at the sound of his voice. Mason was right behind me, and his knuckles brushed my arm as he put his cup in the sink. I drew in a deep breath. My face was right in front of his chest, and he didn't bother taking a step back when I looked up.

"I'm fine." I forced a smile. "Tired. Sorry. It's been a

long day, and there was a lot of wine tonight."

"I warned you that my family are pushers."

"The line-dancing video should have been my first real clue about that."

His lips tugged to one side. "Are you sure you're fine? I don't want to sound like a broken record, but..."

"But what?"

"You don't look fine."

"Are you saying I look miserable?"

"Usually I'd humor you, but right now: yes. You look miserable, Lauren."

"What a charmer," I muttered, tucking my hair behind my ear. "Honestly, I'm just tired. I promise you, that's all it is."

He held his eyes on mine for a long moment before his gaze flicked across my face. "All right. Still, come here."

"For what?"

"This." He pulled me in the way he had earlier tonight. His arms wrapped around my body and held me tight against him.

I wish I could say that I didn't melt against his body, but I did. It was so easy to do, to just slump against his big, strong body like I was supposed to be there. He was rock solid but comfortable, and I all but snuggled right into him as he held me even tighter.

Hugging Mason was like wrapping yourself up into a blanket burrito.

It was like eating a pint of ice cream on day one of your period. Like wearing sweats and no bra while you're eating last night's cold pizza. Like rereading your favorite book or watching your favorite movie for the hundredth time.

Yeah.

He was just…comfortable.

I slid my arms around his waist and closed my eyes. My heart was beating double time in my chest, slamming against my ribs, and the muscles in my stomach were tight and clenched. Tingles danced over my skin, but the place I really felt alive was where his breath fluttered across the top of my head.

It was the same sensation as when someone played with your hair. The little tingles that spread over my scalp made me shiver.

Mason froze.

He felt it.

Uh-oh.

My fingers twitched, digging my nails into his back. The fabric of his shirt bunched against my palm, but I was too afraid to move.

"Cold?" Mason whispered.

I swallowed. "No."

There was no use in lying. It was summer in Florida. A vampire would warm up to human body temps in this weather.

"Then why the shiver?"

"You tickled me. That's all."

"Mhmm."

I bit my lip and dipped my head away from him further, but all I did was bury my face in his chest.

He smelled like beer.

It was not sexy.

He was, though, and that was the problem.

Mason lowered his head so his lips almost brushed my temple. "Feel better?"

I nodded. "Yes. Sorry. I've been hard work today."

"As opposed to the walk in the park you are every other day of the week."

"Hey!" I leaned back in his arms and glared at him. "You're supposed to be nice to me."

He laughed. "I'm always nice to you. I'm the model fake boyfriend."

I sniffed. He really was. "Yes. You'll make some poor woman really happy someday."

His eyes sparkled. That was his only response as he stood there, holding me tight to him, lips twitching into a tantalizing little half-smile.

It did things to me, I won't lie. Swallowing, I squirmed a little to get away from him. I couldn't. It was almost as if he knew exactly what he was doing to me and he was delighting in it.

Damn him.

I was beginning to think that this man was sent to test me.

Well, I wasn't beginning to. He was, because he was testing me.

"You should go," I said, pulling back again. "It's getting late. Knowing my luck, your sister followed us back here and is waiting to see when you'll leave."

He squeezed me, laughing. "Probably. That's the kind of thing Kirsty would do, but I just want to know you're okay."

"I told you, I'm fine."

"Women who say, 'I'm fine,' are never fine."

"Statistically, we are fine at least fifty percent of the time, but we do it to keep you men on your toes."

"Great. More psychology. Is there a part of you that's simple?"

"No. I wouldn't be nearly as interesting as I am if I were easy to figure out."

"True story." His eyes flashed with laughter. "So, is this 'I'm fine' a genuine one or a pretend one?"

"Why would I tell you that?"

"To cut me a fucking break?"

I laughed, pressing my face into his chest. "Why would I want to do that?"

Mason groaned, dropping his head so his chin almost hit his chest. His cheek brushed mine, the rough stubble of his jaw tickling my skin.

It felt good—too good.

I drew in a deep breath and turned my head to the side. My lips were just millimeters from his, and the temptation to move and close the distance was almost overwhelming.

Just to see what it would feel like to kiss him for real.

"Lauren?"

"What?"

"Would you kill me if I broke the rules and kissed you right now?"

"Why don't you find out?"

He hesitated for all of a second before he touched his lips to mine. They were soft and full and warm, and I leaned right into the kiss. My heart thumped inside my chest, and the fabric of his shirt bunched easily inside my hands as I made them into fists.

Mason slipped one hand up my back to cup the back of my neck. I didn't think he could hold me any tighter, but he did, and now our bodies were pressed completely together. The only way we could be any closer would be if we were naked.

Right now, as he sent shivers down my spine, it didn't seem like such a bad idea at all.

He deepened the kiss, flicking his tongue against my lower lip. I moved onto tiptoes to respond, parting my lips for him. He kissed me gently at first, his tongue moving against mine tentatively. When I didn't pull away, he went deeper, kissing me with the kind of passion that sent shivers all over my body.

We kissed for what felt like forever. Night and day could have passed and I would have been oblivious, even though I knew in my mind that it was nothing more than a minute or so.

I was dizzy, like I'd been spun around a thousand times and left to find my own balance. Fiery lust flooded through my veins, and—damn it.

Would it be so bad?

To break the rules?

Just for one night?

In my heart of hearts, I knew the answer was yes.

The only way I could save myself was to stop kissing Mason Jackson. Right now. This very second. Doing anything else; continuing this, doing more, would be nothing short of a very stupid fucking idea.

Yeah, well, someone needed to tell my clitoris that.

Actually, my entire body needed the memo. My hardened nipples, my flushed cheeks, the goosebumps that coated my arms, the hairs that stood on end on the back of my neck—all of me needing telling that this was a very, very bad idea.

This was a bad decision.

I didn't make bad decisions. Well, not regularly. Not like this.

But here I was.

About to throw caution to the wind and pretend like breaking the rules was totally okay. Like we weren't going to walk down a path that potentially gave us a one-way ticket to Regret-ville.

Mason pulled back slowly, dipping to kiss me one last time. "You didn't kill me yet."

I shook my head, raising my gaze to meet his. His eyes look as if they were on fire, blazing with indiscernible feelings that I didn't want to get into and dissect right now.

"Don't say a word about this." I dropped my hands, grabbed his, and pulled him through my apartment toward my room.

"Lauren—"

"I said be quiet." I shoved the door open and pulled him into the room with me. "Before I change my mind."

He raised one eyebrow. "What about the rules?"

"We just broke them. May as well obliterate them entirely for tonight."

"Are you sure?"

"No, I regularly bring men into my bedroom to have sex with them without being entirely certain," I drawled. "I'm starting to think you don't want to have sex with me."

"I didn't say that." He paused. "I just don't want to complicate our relationship."

"Mason, strangers have sex with each other all the time. I think we can both admit that we're attracted to each other—otherwise, you wouldn't have kissed me, and you wouldn't have a third leg in your pants right now."

He adjusted the waistband of his pants. "A third leg. Interesting."

"I didn't bring you in here to talk. My offer only stands for another thirty seconds before I kick you out and take care of myself."

His eyebrow went up again, this time taking his lips with it in a dirty smirk. "Take care of yourself? And you're here snarking about me having an erection."

I folded my arms across my chest. "I'm turned on. I'm not ashamed of that. So, either you do something about it, or I will."

"I suppose we both benefit from this."

"And it's only happening once. I won't offer again. This is literally your only chance to get you some of—"

He cut me off with a swift kiss, yanking me against his body roughly. His hard cock pressed right against me. I wrapped my arms around his neck and kissed him back, grazing my teeth over his lower lip.

He groaned, sliding one hand down to cup my ass. Together, we staggered back toward my bed. My legs hid the side, and we fell down together, laughing between kisses as he covered my body with his.

Every inch of me was ready for this. My dress rode up my thighs when I wrapped them around Mason's waist, pulling him right down on top of me. He was all too happy to oblige.

We kissed, both of us running our hands over the other's body. Mine explored his broad shoulders and strong back down to the hem of his shirt and under while he used one of his hands to steady himself and the other to probe at my thigh.

Together, we sat up. Mason stood and pulled his shirt over his head, revealing a sculpted body from his shoulders to his abs. I wanted to run my tongue along the lines of his muscles, to trace the frame of his abs to commit them to memory.

He pulled me up after him and reached behind me for the zipper to my dress. He slid it down slowly, his fingers trailing over my skin after. I shivered as he reached up and pulled the straps down over my arms, lowering it so it fell to the ground around my feet.

He smirked. A quick, sexy smirk that disappeared in a flash as he kissed me once again. This one was hotter, more desperate. It was a rush of lust and heat through my body as we collapsed together on the bed. It was messy and chaotic, the way he kissed me and ran his hands over my body in exploration.

It was hot and heavy and loaded, from the way he removed his pants to the way he positioned himself so that he could slip his hand between my legs to play with my clit.

I grabbed his neck on both sides and kissed him as his fingers toyed with me. They dipped in and out of my pussy, slicking through my wetness, making my hips buck as I silently pleaded with him for more. He rubbed and teased and played until I could almost taste the brink of my orgasm.

Then he did the asshole thing and pulled his hand away.

"Condom," he said between kisses.

"Drawer."

He got up and moved to the drawer, pulling it open and pulling out the box. "They're out of date."

I shot up to sitting. "What?"

Mason grinned. "Kidding."

I leaned over and slapped his arm. "Don't do that!"

"Why? Were you scared?"

"I happen to take sex seriously. Now shut up, put on that condom, and come over here."

He burst out laughing, but he stripped off his boxers, pulled out a condom, and tore the packet open. I watched a little too intently as he rolled it from the tip of his hard cock down to the base.

Peering over, he smirked.

I shrugged. I wasn't bothered at all. What was I supposed to watch? The TV?

A man putting a condom on was pretty damn sexy.

Mason Jackson doing it was orgasm-inducing.

I reached over and grabbed his hand, pulling him to me. He came easily, pushing me back down when he reached me. My hands ghosted over his body until they reached his neck, then it was my turn to position us.

I opened my legs, and Mason settled between them. His cock pressed against my clit, but he didn't rush. No, he took his sweet-ass time kissing my lips and my jaw and my neck. He took his time running his hands all over my body while he did that, and I swear I was on the brink of screaming.

Finally, he moved.

He slid his hand down between us and after running his fingers through my wetness, he positioned his cock and slowly pushed into me.

Warmth flushed through me. My body responded in an uncontrollable way, and I took a deep breath in as he stilled inside me.

That second was all he gave me. He took my mouth with his, this time vigorously moving his lips across mine as he dipped his tongue against the seam of my lips.

We moved together easily. It was like we'd done it a thousand times before—Mason's thrusts were fast and ferocious, and I responded to him like it was second nature. I tilted my hips, and he went deeper. He fisted my hair, and I offered him my mouth. He dug his fingers into my skin, and I squeezed my legs around his waist.

It didn't take long for my orgasm to hit. It came in a wave of heat and sweat and pure pleasure that rippled through my body. I cried out into Mason's mouth and clenched around him, my entire body going rigid.

He thrust into me, guiding me through it, and when I

was almost done, he groaned out his own release. He buried himself deep inside me as he came, and he fisted my hair so tightly that my scalp stung.

Still, I held onto him, wrapped right around him. It was weirdly comfortable, but that was probably because I was desperately trying to catch my breath as I recovered from the pleasure he'd just given me.

I sighed, sagging down into the mattress.

"All right?" Mason laughed breathily, moving his head so he could meet my gaze.

"Half left, actually," was my equally breathless response.

He laughed, propping himself up on his hands. "Always the joker."

I grinned, but I was sure it was a half-drunk one. Not because I was actually drunk, but because that was how I felt. It was the same sensation as having six tequila shots one after the other.

God bless orgasms.

Mason slowly pulled out of me and stood, taking a few steps back.

I heaved myself over onto my side and onto shaky legs, pushing past him to reach the bathroom first.

"Should I be offended that you can walk?" he shouted through the door.

"No," I called back, dropping onto the toilet. "But what goes up must come down, and I don't want any bodily fluids on my bedroom carpet!"

"So sexy!"

I laughed. It took me a minute to pee and clean myself

up, but when I was done, I grabbed the towel from the rack next to the shower and wrapped it around myself. Opening the door, I stopped and grinned up at him.

He was holding his cock in his hand. It was totally limp, but the condom was still on. "Do you mind?"

"So sexy," I shot back at him.

It was his turn to laugh as he swapped places with me. After changing into some panties and a tank top, I went into the kitchen and poured two glasses of ice water.

Mason appeared a few minutes later wearing his pants with his shirt in his hand.

I looked at it. "Going somewhere?"

He glanced at the shirt. "I wasn't—I didn't want to assume anything."

I walked over to him and handed him his water. "Mason, it's one in the morning. I'm not going to send you home, okay?"

"You almost kicked me out earlier."

"Yeah, well, you've given me an orgasm since then. The least I can do is give you a bed to sleep in." I winked and tapped his cheek. "Turn off the lights, would you?"

CHAPTER SIXTEEN
Mason

I ROLLED OVER, my body colliding with another person.

I froze.

What—

Shit.

Lauren.

It was Lauren.

I was in bed with Lauren.

Because after I'd kissed her last night, she'd marched me into her bedroom and demanded I take care of her horniness before she did it herself.

Fuck me dead, she was something else. She had this confident front—this ballsy, out there persona, but she was hiding a lot. She was hiding a quiet, gentle side of her. I'd almost touched it several times, and I wanted to uncover it.

I wanted to peel back the layers of Lauren Green and see what made her tick.

Because, damn it, I was falling for her.

I didn't want to. I'd tried to fight it. I'd fought myself every step of the way, but here I was, lying in bed next to her, and there was no doubt about it.

My feelings for my fake girlfriend were very, very real.

Stupidly fucking real.

She moved, tilting her head my way. She'd pulled her dark hair into a loose bun on top of her head before we'd gone to bed last night, and it was now a bigger mess than it was then. Dark, loose tendrils framed her face, and a huge chunk of her hair had unwound itself and spread across the pillow.

Her long, dark eyelashes cast a shadow across her cheeks, and when I ran my eyes over her whole face, I smiled at the sight of a zit forming on her chin.

I have no idea why. I just… did.

Her phone buzzed on the nightstand next to her before it emitted a shrill ringing noise that made me wince. Lauren groaned, rolling over. She batted her arm around the air for a moment before it made contact with the nightstand and, on the fifth ring, her phone.

"Hello?" she said groggily into the phone before she realized it was upside down and tried again. "Hello?... What?... Iz, I had a late night. Stop judging me… Eleven? Okay. I'll go. Where's Jared?... Uh-huh, 'kay. I got you. I'll see you there… All right, bye."

She pulled the phone away from her face and jabbed at the screen until it showed that the call was ended. "I didn't sign up for this shit," she muttered, putting the phone down and pulling the covers over her head.

I waited until she stilled, then I moved my foot across the mattress and tickled the back of her foot with my toe.

She screamed, jerking away from me so violently she fell off the bed.

I burst out laughing, falling onto my back.

"Oh, my God! You jerk!" Lauren jumped back onto the bed and shoved at me. "What the hell? Why would you do that?"

"Good morning to you, too," I managed to get out through my chuckles. "You look pretty today."

She leveled me with a glare that said she was not awake enough for my bullshit. "Shut up." She climbed back under the covers, giving me a lame kick for good measure.

"What does a guy have to do around here to get some breakfast?"

"Go looking for the fucking fridge," she muttered into the covers. "Out the door, down the hall, and turn left. Tall silver thing. You can't miss the fucker."

Ah.

"You're a morning person I see."

"So help me, Mason, if you keep fucking talking to me, you'll turn into breakfast."

I rolled over and plastered my body against hers, tugging her right back into me so we were spooning.

"What are you doing?" she murmured.

"Spooning you."

"That's against the rules."

"Yeah, but last night my cock was a good seven inches

inside your body while it broke the rules. I think you can take it pressing against your ass this morning."

She grunted, but she didn't argue any further. She actually snuggled in a little more, not that I let on that I'd felt her do it.

There was something between us; if she didn't want to admit to it right now, that was fine. But her body would give it away, just like it already was.

I didn't know what to do about any of it.

The closest I'd come to getting any kind of emotion out of her was her admission that she was attracted to me.

It was better than nothing.

Her phone rang again, and she swore under her breath as she moved to grab it. "Hello?... Yes, Mom, she called... Of course I'm going... Yes, I know... Mom, she called. I said I'd go. I have to go shower now, okay?... All right, bye."

Lauren threw her phone onto the rug.

"That sounded fun."

"Ugh." She rolled onto her back and looked at me. "My family is hard work."

"Is everything okay?"

She sighed and got up, shoving the covers to the side. "As okay as it can be in my world. My sister's going to the doctor this morning and she wants me to go with her. I suppose I should get ready." She looked over her shoulder at me. "Do you want to take a shower? Do you have to go to work today?"

"No, you're good. I can shower when I get home." I sat up and rubbed my hand through my hair. "Mind if I get some coffee?"

"Help yourself." She tugged the band out of her hair and let it fall down her back. "I won't be long."

She left the room and turned toward the bathroom next door. The sound of the door clicking filled the quiet air, and I got out of bed. I put my pants on and grabbed my shirt before I walked into the kitchen to make coffee.

I made two mugs and left hers on the counter for when she was ready. My phone was on the kitchen island where I'd put it last night, so I grabbed it. The battery blinked at only four percent.

"Shit." I glanced around the kitchen and saw a charging cable plugged in next to the fridge. Thankfully it was the same cable I needed, so I put it into the charge port and leaned against the counter as I checked my messages.

I had a couple from my mom, one from Aunt Pru, and a missed call from my building manager. I decided he was a good place to start, so I dialed his number and waited for him to pick up the phone.

"Mason," came his deep, booming voice. "Sorry to bother you."

"No worries. Is there a problem with my apartment?"

"Mrs. Allerton lodged a complaint this morning. She said she's warned you about noise numerous times, but I knocked on your door and you weren't there."

I frowned. "I'm not home. Haven't been all night. What kind of noise?"

"She said there was a lot of banging and she's fed up of it."

"Was someone knocking at my door? That's her usual

complaint. If I don't get there in a second, she gets up my ass about it."

"I think that's what she said. Were you expecting anyone?"

"I wasn't. Sorry. I have no idea who it could have been."

"All right. Well, other people knocking on your door isn't a crime. I'll tell her we talked and ask her to calm down a little. Thanks, Mason, and sorry I bothered you."

"Don't worry about it, Dan. Thanks." I hung up and shook my head. That fucking woman would be the death of me—if Lauren didn't kill me first.

"Are you okay?" Lauren walked in with a towel twisted on her head.

"Fine. Just my building manager. My neighbor is a pain in the ass. I made you a coffee." I nodded to the steaming mug.

"Thanks." She picked it up and took a sip. "Is that the old lady? The one you told me about before?"

"Yep. Any bit of noise and she complains. It's fine. It's always nothing." I shrugged. "What time do you need to be at the doctor with your sister?"

"About an hour." She put two slices of toast into the toaster. "You want some?"

"Sure. Thanks." I put my phone down and turned. Lauren didn't say anything else. She was intent on keeping her back to me as she busied herself straightening things that didn't need straightening and wiping down countertops that were already perfectly clean.

I tried to hide my grin. For someone who was so ballsy

last night about dragging me into her room, she was real shy right now.

She was desperately trying to avoid eye contact with me. I was desperately trying to make it. It was like a new, weird game that was kinda fun—like a staring contest, but backward.

"Stop staring at me," Lauren said without looking over her shoulder. She grabbed the toast as it popped. "What do you want on your toast?"

"No, and do you have peanut butter?"

"No. I hate peanut butter."

"How can you hate peanut butter?"

"Because I have tastebuds. It's Nutella, strawberry jelly, or butter."

I sighed. "Nutella is fine."

"No." She turned and pointed a knife at me. "Nutella is not fine. Nutella is the nectar of the gods."

"Oh no, are you one of those people who eat it from the jar with a spoon?"

"Only when Mother Nature sends me my monthly love letter." She spread the chocolate onto my toast with a flourish, plated it, and handed it over. "Otherwise, I try to control the urge."

I looked at the toast. "I don't think I'm hungry anymore."

"Was it the monthly love letter thing?"

"Little bit."

"What else should I call it? Shark week? The red river? The hormone war?"

"Just referring to it as your period would suffice." I sat on one of the stools. "And please don't ever say 'the red river' again."

She watched as I bit into my toast. "I thought you said you weren't hungry anymore."

"I wasn't. But I'm a man. I had a moment, but it passed." I tore another piece off with my teeth.

Lauren rolled her eyes as she tugged a stool around slightly and sat down. "Of course it did."

My phone buzzed on the counter, and I leaned over. It was a message from Trevor asking if I wanted to grab a beer tonight. I replied that I did before sitting back down.

Lauren finished her toast before I did. I was about to speak when Henry bounded up onto the counter out of absolutely fucking nowhere and sat on my plate.

"That's okay, Henry. I was finished."

Lauren jolted around. "Oh, my God! Is he sitting on your toast?"

"Yep."

"Henry!" She darted over and grabbed the cat, then lifted him up. "Now you have a Nutella butt!"

"Does that cat ever sit anywhere appropriate?"

"Yes, the window, but only when the sun hits it right. Ugh, now I have to bath him."

"Better you than me."

"Wait, you aren't going to help me?" Her eyes widened.

I finished my coffee and laughed. "No. He's not my cat."

"He sat on your toast!"

"It's not my fault your cat has issues. It's not even an 'If I fits, I sits' situation, Lauren. He just…sits. Whether he fits or not."

She jutted out her lower lip. "Please. Have you ever bathed a cat?"

"No, and I don't ever intend to. I don't even think I like cats."

"How can you not like cats?"

"Easily. I've met yours twice, and he's sat on my head and now, my toast. He's not really trying to endear himself to me."

"Mason, please. Just five minutes. I need to shower off his butt."

"No."

"Please."

"No."

"Pleeeease."

"No. That's the end of it. No."

♥

"You held her cat while she showered him off?" Trev chuckled. "You're whipped, man."

I sighed and rubbed at my arm where Henry had left me with a four-inch-long present. "I'm not whipped. She was just… fucking looking at me with big doe eyes. I couldn't say no."

"You could have, you just chose not to."

"Actually, I did say no. About eight times. She just wore me down."

"Jesus. She's persistent."

I laughed. "You have no idea. It's one of her better traits. Right up there with a never-ending supply of sarcasm and eye-rolls that would start an earthquake."

"She's something else. I don't think I've ever met another woman like her." Trev finished his beer. "Is there anything about her that's simple?"

"No. She's like a little labyrinth. Just when I think I'm breaking her down and finding something out about her, a fucking hedge pops up, and I can't go any further."

He leaned back and motioned for another beer. "I knew this would happen."

"What would?"

"This. You like her."

"'Course I like her. She's a great girl."

"Nah. You like her, Mason. You can tell me that you don't, but it's obvious."

I sighed and switched my empty beer for the full one that the server placed in front of me. "All right—yeah, shit. I do. Can you blame me, though? She's fucking gorgeous, she's hilarious, and she can handle being around my family. It's like the holy trinity of women."

"Hot, funny, and tolerant of old people's bullshit?"

"Exactly. Who wouldn't want to date that?"

He leaned forward on the table. "Here's the thing though, buddy, you don't want to date anyone. Isn't that the tune you've waxed fuckin' lyrical for the last few months?"

He wasn't wrong. I had. It was the one thing I'd insisted on—I didn't want to date. I wasn't ready to date.

But I hadn't been ready for Lauren, either.

Yet here she was, in my life, working her way into my heart bit by bit.

I hadn't been ready for any of this. I hadn't wanted any of this. But I didn't have a say in any of it. It'd just been thrown on me, and I had to go with it.

The biggest problem would be getting Lauren on board with it, too.

"Yeah, it is," I admitted. "I don't want to date, Trev, but I don't think I want to walk away from her either."

"What the fuck do you do, though? You're not in a real relationship. You've both made it clear it'll never be anything more."

I shrugged. "I don't know. I'll think of something. There's a little time. I have her number. I know where she lives. And she owes me for helping her bathe her demon cat."

He snorted. "What are you gonna do? Show up at her door with placards like that dick from that stupid movie?"

"Love Actually?"

"Whatever it's called."

"No. I'm not gonna do that. I'm gonna play it by ear at this point. She's tough to read."

He nodded slowly. "Makes sense. Heard anything else from Claudia?"

"No, but I get the feeling she isn't done with me. She's like a fly around shit."

"She always has been. Your shit, her boss' shit…"

I choked on my beer. "Yeah, yeah. She's just the kind of person who doesn't want you but doesn't want anyone else to have you, either."

"That's called an asshole."

"Well, yeah, but the point stands. She doesn't want me; she just doesn't want Lauren to have me."

"Technically, she doesn't have you."

"I know that. You know that. Claudia doesn't know that."

He leaned forward. "Yeah, but why don't you just not be with Lauren? Claudia would leave you alone then."

I shook my head. "She won't. She's trying to get me back, but that will stop the second she thinks I'm single. It's all games to try to make me do what she wants. She hasn't said a fuckin' word to me since we broke up. Now she's all over me? Nah, she's full of shit."

Trev nodded slowly. "She is. She always has been, though. Lauren is nothing like her." He coughed and rubbed his chin. "Honestly, she's not gonna make it easy for you. It doesn't matter now because you and Lauren aren't really together, but if you go for it with her, it's gonna be a problem."

I sighed. He was right, but I wasn't going to sit here and let my ex control the rest of my life.

I had very fucking real feelings for Lauren. They weren't going to go anywhere anytime soon, not as long as she was in my life. The problem was that I wanted her to stay in my life.

The more time we spent together, the more I fell for

her. The more I wanted to fall for her—even if her cat was a total fucking jerk.

I finished my beer. Trev did the same, setting his glass down on the table. We both threw some money down on the table and headed for the exit.

"See you tomorrow at work?" Trev checked his watch.

"Same as every Monday," I replied, pulling my phone from my pocket. There was a missed call from an unknown number but no message, so I cleared the notification and put it back in my pocket.

I waved him goodbye and turned toward my apartment. It was only a couple of blocks, and it didn't take me long to get from the bar to my place. I dug my keys out and let myself in, then took the stairs up to my apartment.

And froze.

"What the hell are you doing here again?"

The blonde woman outside my apartment turned, and Claudia looked back at me. "Can we talk?"

CHAPTER SEVENTEEN
Lauren

"SO, I LIKE HIM." I poured wine into my glass. "Obviously, this is a problem."

Tina took the bottle when I was done with it. "I don't see the problem. He's hot. He's a nice guy. He makes you laugh. Why would pursuing something real with him be bad?"

"Because she's a grumpy bitch," Madi said, taking the bottle and finishing it off in her glass. "She banged the guy last night, but today is the problem?"

I rolled my eyes. "Look, it was a lapse in judgment."

"No, it wasn't. It was an excellent idea. If you get the opportunity to sleep with such a fine specimen, you should damn well do it."

"Put your vagina away," Tina said. "Lauren, it wasn't a bad choice. You had sex with him. So what? What is the worst that could happen? He says no? He obviously likes you."

Madi grinned. "One part of him does, anyway."

I threw a cushion at her. "Shut your face."

"Just do it," Madi continued. "You're not fake breaking up yet anyway. It might naturally become something. If you get along that well, it's not out of the realm of possibility."

"She's right," Tina said, hugging a cushion to her chest. "Let it happen as it happens. It's not going to be the end of the world, and don't you dare tell me you don't want a relationship."

"I don't want a relationship!" I protested. "I'm happy being single. Really, I am. I'm not going to go and look for a relationship."

"You're not looking for one! It found you, idiot."

"I don't care. I don't want the hassle of having a man around." Never mind that he was helpful when Henry had a Nutella ass. "They require attention. I already have a cat for that. And a sister. And my mother."

Madi snorted. "Okay, look—you have, what? Two weeks-ish left of this fake-relationship stuff?"

"Pretty much."

"So deal with it. Just roll with it. He's not high maintenance, is he?"

I shrugged one shoulder. "Not really."

"There you go. He's not needy. He makes you laugh. He's good in bed. That's all you need in a man."

"A stable job and loyalty are also up there," Tina added. "Nobody wants an unfaithful, broke bastard."

"Fair point." Madi nodded.

I sighed and sipped my wine. "Yes, yes, Mason is perfect. Can we move on now?"

They both squealed.

"I've never heard you call a guy perfect!" Tina clapped her hands, startling Henry, who was sleeping on the windowsill.

He jerked his head up and, with a lazy blink, bounded over to the sofa where she was sitting and promptly sat on her head.

"I asked for this, didn't I?" Her eyes flicked between us both.

"Yep." Madi leaned forward and passed her her wine glass. "At least you can drink now."

I laughed, only just avoiding snorting wine up my nose. "You totally asked for it. You know better than to wake him up."

Henry meowed.

"So what are you going to do?" Tina pushed her hair out of her face, only for Henry to move his leg and push it all back over her eye again.

"Nothing," I said honestly. My phone buzzed, and I reached for it on the coffee table. "I don't see that I have to actively do anything. I mean, if something is meant to happen, then it'll happen, right?"

"You're spending too much time on Pinterest with that philosophical shit," Madi said.

"Whatever. Look, I'm not going to actively pursue anything. I don't even know if he actually likes me. I mean, I offered myself to him like he was an old English king, and

I was a pig with an apple in my mouth. And he hesitated."

Tina tapped her chin. "Maybe he didn't want to make it awkward."

"He'd just had his tongue halfway down my throat. It was awkward."

"So awkward," Madi agreed. "Okay. So you're just going to let the chips fall where they may?"

"Yeah. That's what people do, isn't it? When they date? They let everything fall into place." I shrugged and opened the new message on my phone.

> UNKNOWN: I saw your ad online. Are your services still available?

Huh.

I looked at Madi and Tina. "Guys, did I ever take down that ad? Offering my dating services?"

They shared a glance. "I don't think so," Tina answered. "Why?"

"Because I just got this text." I read out the message. "I can't have taken it down."

Madi bit her lip. "I guess you didn't. Ask and see if that's what they mean. For all you know, someone with your number put up a sex ad or something."

"If anyone was going to do that, it would be you," I pointed out before I replied.

> LAUREN: Do you mean the fake date ad?
>
> UNKNOWN: Yes. Are you still available? I need a date for tomorrow night. It's my dad's engagement party.

I read out that text then said, "What do I do?"

Tina moved so quickly she actually dislodged the hefty lump of feline on top of her head. Henry mewled his displeasure as he headed toward my bedroom.

"What do you mean, what do you do? You say no!" She waved her hands. "Lauren!"

"Eh." Madi leaned back and dangled her wine glass between her fingers.

"Eh? What is *eh*?" Tina's eyes bugged out of her head.

Madi tucked her red hair behind her ear. "I don't know that it's a bad thing. She's clearly torn about how she feels about Mason and, more to the point, there's nothing that says she can't do it. They're not actually seeing each other. She can do what she wants."

I glanced down at my phone. She had a point, but… "It feels weird. Like, not the actual fake date thing, but the situation. Kirsty saw my ad for the joke it was—kind of—and messaged me on behalf of Mason. Why would any sane guy think that was serious?"

"Guys are weird," Madi said. "If you don't feel comfortable, Lauren, don't do it. Say you're busy."

"She's right." Tina set her empty glass on the coffee table. "Or, if you want, we'll go with you. It's Monday tomorrow, right? You have the early shift."

I bit the inside of my cheek. She was right—I did. I'd be off by eight, and if I took them both with me… "You'd go with me?"

"Of course," they said simultaneously.

"Ugh. I feel like a pig heading to slaughter." I sniffed and hit the reply button.

LAUREN: What time & where? I have to work until 8.

UNKNOWN: The train station at 8:15?

LAUREN: Okay, but that doesn't give me time to change.

UNKNOWN: It's ok. I'm coming from work too.

LAUREN: K, see you then.

"Okay." I relayed the messages to the girls. "Are you sure you can both do this?"

They nodded.

"Are you sure you want to do this?" Tina asked me, concern flashing in her eyes. "You don't look comfortable with this."

"I'm not," I admitted. "Something doesn't feel right, but not in a jogger-in-a-dark-park kind of way."

Madi snorted. "What kind of way?"

"Jogger-in-a-dark-park," I repeated. "It's always joggers who find dead bodies in parks. It's why they can't be trusted."

"Fair enough."

"It just feels weird." I finished my glass and set it down. "I don't know why. I just don't think I like it very much, but at the same time, that's exactly why I have to go."

Tina hauled herself up with a sigh. "You're gonna get yourself murdered one day, girl."

"Yeah, well, as long as you don't start jogging, you won't ever have to find me."

She snorted, hitting me on the side of the head as she

made her way to the bathroom. "Lauren!" she called back to us.

"What?"

"Your cat is sitting on the toilet."

♥

The more I thought about this, the worse the idea became.

Not because of Mason.

In fact, this was a good thing where he was concerned. I was going to swear that until I was blue in the face. We weren't actually dating, none of this was real, and I could go out with whoever I wanted, right?

Right.

In theory.

In reality, the guilt was powerful. I felt as though I was going behind his back, and it was a hard feeling to shake off. I didn't want to betray him, even though I technically wasn't.

Was that why this whole thing felt 'off?'

Because my stupid little heart had caught the feelings flu?

Ugh.

I didn't even know anymore. My confusion was real. It was consuming, and if I didn't pull up my big girl panties soon, I was going to be screwed big time.

I took a deep breath and leaned against the streetlight. The train station was lit up, bright and lively, and there was a slow but steady stream of people coming in and out.

I had no idea who I was looking for, and I was counting almost entirely on them recognizing me.

I was wearing a hot pink sweater. It wasn't going to be that hard to notice me.

I glanced over toward the train station café where Tina and Madi were sitting, each nursing a cup of coffee. Madi shot me a thumb up of reassurance, and I forced my gaze away from them.

God, what was I doing?

It was too late to back out of this now.

It was eight-fifteen, and my mystery date was about to show up.

I was insane. I'd lost my damn mind.

I pulled my phone from my pocket and looked down at the screen. There were no new messages, no missed calls, nothing. My stomach sank, and I didn't even know why—it wasn't like I was expecting anything from anyone.

Jesus, what was happening to me?

"Lauren?"

My head jerked up at the sound of a voice—a woman's voice.

A familiar woman's voice.

My gaze rested on a face I honestly never wanted to see again in my life.

Claudia.

Kill her with kindness, Lauren. Do not fling your shoe at her.

"Can I help you?" I kept my tone level.

"As a matter of fact, you can." A smile that reeked of

slyness spread across her face. "I'm your date for tonight."

"I'm sorry?"

"The little ad you put up online." Her smile widened, and she put one hand on her hip. "I'm the person who texted you."

My stomach flipped. "I don't understand."

"How much clearer do I need to say it? I'm the one who texted you. Your ad is still up. The ad you conveniently posted right before my high school reunion." Smugness flashed in her eyes, and she adjusted the strap of her expensive purse. "I know you and Mason aren't really together. It's all a ruse, for a reason I don't understand. I'm not going to even try."

"Why are you here?" I asked, a bite to my tone. "You don't know anything about me and Mason. That ad doesn't mean anything."

"Doesn't it?"

"I don't have to explain anything to you, Claudia. You're his ex."

"You're right. I am his ex." She looked me up and down. "The ex who was at his apartment last night."

I wanted to respond.

I really, really did. I had an entire arsenal of comebacks for women like Claudia—ones who thought they were better than everyone else, who thought they were the dog's balls, who had themselves so high up on their horses that they could barely see the ground.

Yet nothing came out.

My lips parted, but no words escaped. Nothing. Not even a squeak of annoyance.

Her words were a sucker punch to the gut. Why? I couldn't pinpoint that right now. I knew her type—they were jealous and manipulative, and chances were, what she was saying was a crock of bullshit.

Mason hated her.

In my rational mind, I knew that.

The rest of me, though? It stung.

I had no right to feel this way. I'd come here thinking I was going to be another guy's date. I didn't get to take the high road right now.

Claudia took a step closer toward me, and that was all I needed to find my voice again.

"Did you really?" I drawled. "And I'm sure he invited you in for cake and coffee and a good old catch-up, did he?"

"Not exactly cake and coffee, but a catch-up?" She smirked. "Let me tell you—that's how I *know* you aren't together."

I wanted to claw out her eyes.

"I'm going to give you ten seconds to run before I slap that smirk off your face and catapult it into orbit," I warned her. Out of the corner of my eye, I could see Madi and Tina rushing over to me.

Claudia's eyes flashed. "You wouldn't dare. Your precious fake boyfriend wouldn't like that."

"Actually, he'd pay for a front row seat," I said through gritted teeth. "Because before you run your mouth at me about our relationship being fake, maybe you should call him right now and see where he was until just before lunch yesterday."

Her nostrils flared right as Madi and Tina joined me. "I don't think so."

"No, neither did I. Because regardless of anything else, you and I both know he won't answer your call." It was my turn to look her over head to toe. "Green isn't your color, Claudia. Give it up."

"I don't have to give up. All I have to do is tell everyone your relationship isn't real and show them the ad. Then this little *relationship* will be over."

"Go ahead," I replied in a withering tone. "Seriously. Be my guest. You'll save us both a job of pretending to break up."

With that, I turned my back on her and stormed past my best friends. They followed me without hesitation, but I didn't stop until we were in the parking lot where we'd parked a block away.

I unlocked my car and got in. My blood boiled—she'd tricked me, and now that was it. That was the end of it.

It was the end of me and Mason.

The end of anything that could possibly happen.

And that—that was the reason for the sinking in my stomach. The coiling I felt deep inside. That pure anger and frustration that threatened to boil over the surface.

Fuck me dead, I hated that woman.

How petty did she have to be? Could she really not let him go? I'd understand if he'd broken up with her, but that wasn't the case. She was the one who'd broken up with him. She'd done the dirty on him.

What was her problem? Was she really just that horrible of a person?

"That was interesting," Madi said from the passenger seat.

"Who was she?" Tina added from the back.

I took a deep breath in through my nose before I huffed it back out. "Claudia. Mason's ex."

"Ohhh," they both said. "That makes sense," Madi added. "I could smell the estrogen from the café."

I tutted and turned the key in the ignition. "She's impossible. I don't know what she thinks she's playing at."

Tina clicked her belt in. "What did she say?"

"She implied she was with Mason last night. Like, with-with him."

"With him how you were on Saturday night? Bumping uglies? Sending the train into the tunnel?"

"Enough," I snapped. "Sorry. I just—ugh. I don't know why I feel like this. I don't like her, but I feel like I could kick a wall right now."

"Ah, jealousy," Madi said, examining her nails. "Admit it. You have a lot more feelings for Mason than you thought. It's not surprising since you get along so well."

I wasn't going to admit that right now. "She knows our relationship isn't real."

"We know," Tina said. "We were there when you told her to tell Mason's family."

I dropped my head onto the steering wheel. It hit the horn, and the ear-screeching sound rang out until Madi leaned forward and sat me up again.

"She won't do anything tonight, because she's a manipulator. She'll get you when you least expect it. I wouldn't be surprised if she showed up at his door in the next thirty minutes."

I groaned, leaning back right in my seat. "What do I do?"

"You have to tell Mason. Right now."

I pulled out my phone and brought up our last text conversation. She was right. I knew I had to tell him, even if I wasn't looking forward to the part of the conversation where I told him how and why we'd come to have the conversation.

Being an adult sucked sometimes.

I pulled out my phone and brought up our text chat and typed four simple words.

LAUREN: We need to talk.

CHAPTER EIGHTEEN
Lauren

"SSH. SSH. IT'S OKAY. It's okay." I gently patted Cara's back as she petered off with her tears. She'd already vomited on me twice and given me a poop explosion, and if I were a worse sister, I'd wonder what the hell I was doing here.

All right, so I was. I was wondering why I'd insisted on taking my baby niece for the day when I could barely look after myself at this point in my life.

Well, I knew why. My sister being diagnosed with postpartum depression was the whole reason for our emergency doctor visit on Sunday, and now, on this bright and airy Tuesday, here I was.

Lauren Poppins.

Mary was way better than I'd ever be.

Jared was away working, and Iz was so overwhelmed

with everything that I'd basically shown up first thing this morning and demanded she pack up all the baby things so she could have a break. She'd already texted me that she'd taken a three-hour nap, a one-hour bath, and gotten the laundry done without being thrown up on.

Cara finally settled after another ten minutes of rocking and walking around the room. I was pretty sure there was a good amount of spit-slash-vomit down my back, but I was a little past caring. She was quiet, and that was all that really mattered right now.

Even Henry had taken cover in the linen cupboard.

But she was finally quiet. She was down, sleeping soundly on my shoulder. I blew out a long sigh of relief. I knew babies were hard work—I did—but I didn't realize just how much until right now.

Two knocks thundered at my door, and I both grimaced and winced at the same time. Thankfully, Cara didn't seem to be bothered by it, so I rocked her as I made my way to the apartment door and swung it open.

Mason stood on the other side. He'd clearly come straight from work because his jeans were ripped and dirty and dusty, and there were flecks of sawdust in his hair. I couldn't help but grin at the sight of him, especially when he caught sight of the tiny human resting against my shoulder.

He raised one eyebrow. "Something I should know?"

I covered my mouth before I laughed too loudly. "No, it's my niece. Come in." I moved back for him. "My sister's appointment over the weekend was an emergency one. They diagnosed her with postpartum depression, so I told her I'd take Cara for the day until I have to work in a couple hours."

"That's sweet of you. Is she doing okay?"

Ugh, why was he so kind? "She's fine. She's not covered in poop or vomit unlike me, so she's probably feeling better." I grinned. "Let me put her down and change my shirt, and then we can talk."

"Right. Do you mind if I make a coffee? Do you want anything?" He paused at the kitchen island.

"No, and yes, a coffee. Please." I smiled and carried Cara through to my room where her bed was temporarily set up. After making sure she was safe, I changed my shirt and gave myself a quick once-over for traces of vomit.

Finding none, I sprayed myself with deodorant and pulled the door closed behind me.

Look—vomit lingered, okay?

"Here." Mason handed me a cup the second I stepped back into the living room. "You look like you need it spiked with whiskey, though."

I laughed and leaned against the counter. "Babies are hard. Like really hard. And messy!"

His lips twitched.

"This is my third shirt today, and I don't even have leaky boobs as an excuse. Nope. Just vomit. People tell you babies are hard work but fuck me dead." I shook my head. "My poor clothes."

"Of course they're hard work. They rely on you for everything."

"Obviously, I know that. You just underestimate how long everything takes. Getting my mail earlier took me twenty minutes, and I didn't even have to leave the building!" I cradled my mug and raised my eyebrows. "You know what's false advertising? Those baby commercials on TV where it's all sweetness and light and chubby-toe kissing. It's all shitty backs and spittle in your hair."

He dropped his head. His entire body shook with silent laughter, and I pursed my lips.

"Thanks for the support."

"You're welcome." Mason grinned. "What did you want to talk about?"

My smile dropped like a lead balloon. "Uh—you wanna sit down?"

His eyebrows shot up. "It's like that, is it? Is this where you fake break up with me?"

"No! I mean, maybe?" I frowned. "You might fake break up with me."

"Oh, shit. Okay." He put down his mug. "What happened?"

I swallowed. There was a big lump in my throat, and it tasted a lot like regret, even though I had nothing to regret, did I?

I did, and I knew I did. Even if it didn't bother Mason at all.

"Okay. Sunday night, when the girls were here, I got a text."

"Right."

"Apparently, I'm an idiot who forgot to take down my ad from the internet."

"I think I see where this is going." He leaned back against the counter and folded his arms across his chest. "Did you fake cheat on me?"

"No! Can you let me finish my story?"

He waved his arm. "Go on."

"So kind of you," I snarked. "Anyway, I didn't feel right about going, so I took Tina and Madi with me."

"They're your best friends, right?"

"Yes. I thought you were letting me finish."

He just stared at me.

Men.

"We arranged to meet after I finished work last night. They said they needed a date for their dad's engagement party."

"And you didn't think a Monday night was a weird night to have an engagement party?"

I paused. "I didn't think at all, to be honest."

"Well, at least you can admit that."

"Hey. There's no need to insult me."

He half-smiled. "Carry on."

"Turned out, it wasn't actually a date. It was Claudia."

Mason froze. "What?"

"Yeah. It was Claudia." I grimaced. "She found the ad and pretended to need a date to get me there. She told me she knew our relationship wasn't real, and she said she was going to tell your family that we're faking it."

"All right." He rubbed his chin.

"She also tried to tell me that she'd been at your place on Sunday night."

"She was."

It was my turn to still. "What?"

"She was at my apartment on Sunday night." He put down his mug and gripped the edge of the counter. "It's not the first time she's shown up since the reunion. I know of three times for sure, but I think it was more."

My eyebrows shot up.

I was pissed.

I had no business being pissed, but here I was, getting all kinds of angry.

"Three times, huh?"

Mason's lips pulled to one side. "You look a little more bothered about that than I expected."

"Bothered? I'm not bothered. You can do what you want with your ex. I think it's a little shitty to sleep with us both on the same day, but that's your prerogative."

He stared at me for a moment before he laughed. "You think I slept with you both on the same day?"

I pursed my lips. "Well, not really."

"Do you really think I'm that kind of guy?"

"No." I sighed. "But it would be so much easier to justify this annoyance if you were."

"What annoyance?"

"Why do you look so happy about me being annoyed?"

"I'm not happy. I'm pleasantly surprised."

"That I'm in a bad mood? You're a sick, sick man."

He pushed off the side and walked over to me. "Listen to me, Lauren. Claudia is a master manipulator. She cheated on me, but she doesn't want anyone else to have me. She's showing up at my place, putting on puppy dog eyes, and hoping she can talk me into getting back together with her. I'd bet that her relationship with her boss isn't going too well, and she wants a backup guy."

I looked up at him.

"It's not going to happen." His voice was firm—tough, yet still weirdly gentle at the same time. "I have zero interest in her. So whatever she told you, it was a lie."

"You didn't do anything with her?"

"I barely had a conversation with her. The first time, I basically kicked her straight out. I humored her on Sunday by letting her spew her bullshit, then did the same thing again." He put one hand on the island. "I'd bet she'd already found the ad, and she messaged you after she'd left. She's probably thinking she can use it to manipulate me into dating her again."

"I hate her."

"Yeah, well, take a number and get in line." His blue eyes sparkled with silent laughter. "Personally, I don't give a crap if she tells my family it was fake. Kirsty set this up. Aunt Pru was complicit in the deception. We can totally blame it all on them."

A small smile teased my lips. "You're not fake breaking up with me."

"Not today." He tapped me on the nose. "Besides, we both know this isn't all entirely fake anymore."

My heart skipped. "What do you mean?"

"I can't decide if you're being deliberately dense or if I should just humor you."

"Guess and find out."

"There's more than just attraction between us, Lauren. I think it'd be easier for us both if we just admit that we're starting to feel something real."

My tongue darted out to wet my lips. "I don't—um."

He raised one eyebrow. "Go ahead. Tell me I'm wrong. I'll wait."

"You're wrong," I said weakly.

"That was lame. Try again."

I spun on the stool and got up, running my fingers through my hair. "Fine. What if you're right? Neither of us wants a relationship, Mason. I don't think that's changed just because we get along as well as we do. Unless you've suddenly changed your mind overnight."

"I didn't say that, did I? There's more between us than just a sexual attraction. We can lie about it all we like, but it's not going to change anything."

"I quite like lying to myself. I'm rather adept at living in denial. It's why I don't go to the gym anymore. I can convince myself the cake I ate last night didn't contribute to my love handles."

"What love handles?"

"Good response."

"Thank you. Can you stop avoiding the point of the conversation now?"

"I'm not avoiding anything."

"You're avoiding everything."

"I disagree."

"Then we agree to disagree." He stalked over to me and stopped right in front of me, one hand reaching out. His fingers brushed my skin as he pushed my hair behind my ear, and they traced a trail down the side of my neck.

"Would it be that bad?" he asked in a low voice. "If this turned into something more?"

I didn't reply.

"I have feelings for you, Lauren. Real feelings. I don't care where they came from or the reason they're able to exist in the first place. I don't care that this relationship is fake—because nobody else ever doubted that it was anything other than real. Doesn't that tell you something?"

I opened my mouth to speak, but nothing came out.

It did. It told me a lot of things. It told me that nobody has doubted us. Nobody has looked at us and thought, "Fucking hell, they're awkward together." That somehow we pulled this thing off, no matter how many physical boundaries we set.

Of course, we'd broken past them all in private, but whatever.

Even without being all over each other, without putting on a display of affection for everyone to see, we still convinced them that our relationship was real.

That was a job well done.

And one that told me more than I was willing to accept.

Like the fact that this fake relationship could potentially be a very successful real one if we'd let it. If *I* would let it.

I cleared my throat and turned my face away, but Mason captured my face in his hands. His grip was so steady and firm that I had no choice but to meet his eyes. They were a mass of emotion; determination and uncertainty and raw feelings that I wish I'd never seen.

He dipped his head and pressed his lips against mine.

They were warm and soft, just like I remembered from two nights ago, except this time he smelled like sawdust and fresh air.

I leaned into him, squeezing my eyes shut tight.

"You feel that. I know you do," he said in a low voice against my lips. "I'm not crazy, Lauren. There's something about you that I don't think I can give up."

"That'll be the sarcasm. It's scintillating."

"For the love of—"

"What?"

He dropped his hands and stepped back. "You'll die before you admit the truth, won't you?"

"No." I took my own step back from him. "I can't admit it, Mason. I can't tell you how I really feel, because if I do, then I can't walk away from this."

"I'm not walking away from it. I'm not walking away from what I know is between us."

"If I tell you how you make me feel, it'll give you the power to break my heart. I have no desire to give anyone that power."

"And what if you don't tell me? What if you keep it all to yourself, and in two weeks, when we put an end to the charade we began, you break your own heart because you were too fucking stubborn to admit the truth?"

"I—" *Had not thought that far ahead.* "All right, say I admit it. Say I tell you I have feelings for you that are way too real for my liking. What happens then? Your darling ex tells your family we've been faking it and now we have to convince them it's real? Nobody is going to believe us!"

"Oh, fuck me—Lauren, it doesn't matter!" Mason ran

his hand through his hair. "I don't owe anyone but you anything. I don't owe my mother, my sister, my aunt, my grandpa—I don't owe them a single fucking thing where my relationships are concerned. The only person I give a shit about is you. You are the only person I want to convince about us."

Silence passed between us for a minute. The longest minute ever. Until I dipped my head to look at the floor and said, "I'm not *un*convinced, okay? I'm reluctant. There's a difference."

He rolled his eyes. "That's basically the same thing in this context."

"How is it?"

"Because you're unwilling to open your eyes to reality and admit the truth," he said firmly.

"I'm not unwilling. Why is being hesitant such a bad thing? It's all fun and games when we're pretending, but what if this screws up when it's real? We get along just fine when we're nothing more than friends."

"You won't know unless you give it a chance."

"Giving it a chance scares me."

"I know. It scares me, too." He came back to me. "Remember how my last relationship ended? Claudia made me never want to be with anyone ever again, but then I met you. And, Lauren? I don't want to be in a relationship with just anyone. I want to try and make things work with you."

I peered up at him through my eyelashes. "What if it doesn't?"

"Then it doesn't. But I think it's worth giving it a shot." He half-smiled at me. "You're beautiful. You're funny. And I already know you're a huge pain in the ass, so it's not like that's going to scare me off."

I covered my face with my hands and laughed.

He pulled me into a bear hug and pressed his lips to the top of my head. "Come on. It'll be fun."

"What will be?"

"A date. Let's go on one date, and if it's really weird, we'll amicably break up or admit the ruse. If it goes well, we'll officially try being in a relationship."

"Okay, while I appreciate your logic, there's a fundamental flaw in it all."

"What's that?"

"We've technically already been on the dates. We've already done the getting to know each other part of dating."

He raised an eyebrow. "How so?"

"Well, there was the reunion where we got a burger right after. Technically the lunch meeting to discuss our fake relationship could be classified as a date, and so could the time you came over here and showed me the crazy videos from your family. The two family events we went to together are dates, and Saturday night was definitely an extension of a date."

"Ah, Saturday night, when you told me complete strangers sleep together and it doesn't mean a thing."

"Total strangers do sleep together without it meaning a thing." I shuffled my feet. "But sometimes it can mean something."

"You dragged me into your bedroom."

"Oh, my God. I dragged you in because I was hoping you'd screw my brains out. Stop making a big deal out of it."

"Did I?"

"What?"

"Did I screw your brains out?"

"If I admit that you did, do I still have to admit that I have feelings for you?"

I froze.

A grin spread across Mason's face. "Well, well, well," he said slowly. "Where did that come from?"

I took a deep breath in through my nose and stared him down. "You should probably go now."

"No." He pulled me in and kissed me before I could protest. Any half-hearted attempt I had left died when he wrapped his arm around my waist and held me flush against his body.

I gave in to him. It wasn't the worst feeling in the world, to be kissed by him. In fact, it was one I could get used to.

"So what happens now?" Mason murmured. "If we've determined that we've already done the first date things and that we both like each other, now what?"

I opened my mouth to tell him that I didn't know, but I was saved by the bell.

The bell being a ten-pound human being with lungs the size of a grown adult.

I grimaced and patted his chest. "Well, I need to return Cara to my sister and go to work. I'd say you could stay, but Henry's been looking for a head to sit on for hours, and he's out for revenge since I kicked him out of Cara's bed."

Mason shuddered as he let me go. "I'll pass. I'll bring

him tuna next time I come over and that should endear him to me."

"Good luck with that!" I called over my shoulder.

CHAPTER NINETEEN

Lauren

MASON: She told my mom.

I blinked at the message on my screen.

Oh, shit.

LAUREN: When???

MASON: Today. She stopped in at her work specifically to tell her, then showed her screenshots.

LAUREN: Fuck a duck.

MASON: I've been summoned for a chat.

LAUREN: I have to work. Oh no. What a shame.

MASON: Don't worry, I've got it. I'll handle her.

LAUREN: What are you going to tell

her?

MASON: The truth. And I'm going to drop Kirsty right in the middle of it.

LAUREN: Well, it is her fault. If you look past my terrible decision regarding the ad.

MASON: I don't think it was that much of a bad idea.

LAUREN: You hated the entire thing at first.

MASON: Yeah, but I didn't know how annoyingly delightful you are then. A few hours in your company would make a monk give up the church, never mind a grouchy builder.

LAUREN: A monk couldn't handle me. He'd run back to his hut before the bill was delivered.

MASON: Monks don't live in huts.

LAUREN: Do I look like an encyclopedia?

MASON: You usually have an answer for everything.

LAUREN: Why are you such a fucking smartass?

MASON: I've been taking tips from you. Picking things up here and there. It looks like it's paying off.

LAUREN: Hardy har-har-har, aren't you the funny man?

MASON: Given how much you laugh around me, yes, I am the funny man.

LAUREN: We're going to need to break up. I don't think I can cope with another smartass in my life. I'm enough work as it is.

MASON: You'll get used to it. This smartass comes equipped with the ability to provide orgasms.

LAUREN: Oh, honey, did nobody teach you about masturbation when you were younger?

MASON: One day, you're going to get yourself off, and then I'm going to get you off, and we'll compare notes.

LAUREN: I am not taking notes on an orgasm.

LAUREN: Also, we've gotten off track.

MASON: At least you can hide when you've gotten off track.

MASON: But yes, you're right. Let's get back to it.

LAUREN: What are you going to tell your mom when you're done blaming everything on your sister?

MASON: The truth. I'll tell her that we've talked about it and we're going to date for real, but she's going to back off because we're going to do it in our own time.

LAUREN: Aunt Pru will be delighted.

MASON: No. We aren't telling Aunt Pru or she'll start buying those wedding books.

LAUREN: It's okay. I have a plan.

MASON: Oh, yeah? What's what?

LAUREN: I'll tell her she needs to set Kirsty up with someone, then we'll make her an online dating account and find her someone.

MASON: That's mean.

MASON: I like it. Seems like the kind of thing my future wife should do.

LAUREN: Wash out your mouth, buster. I haven't tasted your cooking yet. I already told you that's the dealbreaker, especially now you won over Henry with your fancy fucking tuna.

MASON: Henry's misunderstood, that's all.

LAUREN: He's misunderstood where he's supposed to sit. I don't need the two of you conspiring against me. My life is stressful enough.

MASON: Why now? Is your mom calling

you again?

LAUREN: No, my sister is texting me daily updates on her hemorrhoids. I know more about her anal region than I do my own.

MASON: I don't really know what to say to that.

LAUREN: Nobody does.

LAUREN: What time do you want me to come over tonight?

MASON: When do you finish work?

LAUREN: Eight-thirty.

MASON: Why don't you come over then?

LAUREN: All right, but I'm wearing yoga pants to work tonight. You've been warned.

MASON: It's fine. I bet your ass looks great in yoga pants.

LAUREN: You are not wrong.

CHAPTER TWENTY
Mason

"I JUST DON'T understand why you'd fake a relationship, Mason." My mother looked at me disapprovingly over the rim of her martini glass. "Look—you're driving me to drink early!"

Yeah, I was the reason for that.

"Okay—this isn't on me." I leaned back on the sofa and crossed my legs at my ankles. "Let me tell you what actually happened, from the beginning."

"Please do."

"Lauren put an ad up online. It was a joke with her friends after girls' night, and Kirsty responded to her post. We texted after that—I was going to shut it down, but it was the reunion. She was happy to go and get under Claudia's skin, and I didn't really care either way." I ran my hand through my hair. "It was only supposed to be one date, then Kirsty dropped us in the shit at dinner."

"Watch your language," Mom said firmly. "The dinner—oh! She was lying then?"

"Yeah. You were so excited, I didn't have the heart to tell you she was being a pain, so I texted Lauren after and asked her to go along with it for a few weeks."

Mom sighed. "Sweetheart, you didn't have to do that. I was excited that you might have found someone, but I wish you'd been honest."

"I don't. I'm glad I lied. If I hadn't, we wouldn't have spent any time together."

Her eyebrows shot up. "What do you mean?"

"We get along really, really well. We have the same sense of humor, we like the same things, and we just enjoy spending time together." I shrugged. "We're going to see where things go."

"Would you have told me if Claudia didn't?"

"No," I said honestly. "You wouldn't have needed to know, and neither would anyone else. I love you, Mom, and I respect you more than you know, but I told Lauren that the only person I need to justify my feelings to is her, and I stand by that."

"I can respect that," Mom replied, putting her martini glass on the side table. "I know that who you date is none of my business, Mase, but I just want you to be happy. Sometimes that can come across as me meddling, but it's not what I'm trying to do."

"I know. And hey, this time it all worked out. Even if me and Lauren don't work out, I won't regret it. I forgot what it was like to have fun with someone else."

"Good. I'm glad. It sounds like Claudia's attempt at breaking you up backfired."

"It was never going to be successful, Mom. I'm not interested in her anymore. Nothing she says or does is going to make me ever want her again." I sat up straighter and shrugged. "Sorry we lied to you."

"Sweetheart, I told you; don't worry about it. It's all good. As long as you were happy with what you were doing… Well, you didn't cause any harm, did you? And on the bright side, you know Lauren can handle our crazy family. There won't be any surprises at the next big party."

"You know, this family could stand to have a few casual, quiet get-togethers once in a while."

"We could, but then we wouldn't get any incriminating videos for the future. Nobody ever did anything embarrassing while sitting around the television and eating Thai food."

"Well…"

"We are not discussing my birthday last year."

I laughed. "Please."

"No, Mason. Listen to me—forget my birthday. I'm glad we got this cleared up. I'm going to have a word with your sister about her meddling in your life and running her mouth."

"Aunt Pru knew, too."

"Yes, well, Pru is in a world of her own. She can do what she likes."

I grinned. "You know she'll kick your ass."

"That's enough of you." She skirted to the edge of the sofa and motioned for me to shoo. "Go and be useful somewhere."

"You called me here," I reminded her as I stood up.

"And now I'm getting rid of you. Off you go. Bye, son."

I laughed as I made my way to the front door. "Bye, Mom!" I heard her laughter echo through the house as I stepped outside and made it to my truck. When I was safely in there, I pulled out my phone and texted Lauren.

> MASON: Crisis averted. My mother is happy with our newfound relationship.

Her response was surprisingly fast.

> LAUREN: We'll see how your food tastes. Then we'll talk about relationships.

♥

Lauren gasped, her nails digging into my shoulders as her back arched beneath me.

I gripped her thigh even tighter and moved inside her, thrusting my cock into her wet pussy harder than I had before. Her moans of pleasure as she writhed beneath me were straight out of a wet dream, and if her nails weren't slicing into my skin so firmly, I'd say that it was a fucking wet dream.

Jesus, she felt so damn good.

We moved together until my balls went so tight that I knew I was about to come. I gritted my teeth as I held onto the sensation. I wasn't going to go before she did—I was determined to hold it back until I couldn't any longer.

It was fucking painful. All I wanted to do was come,

but she was so close. So close that I couldn't let go.

Instead of focusing on how badly I wanted to come, I focused on her. On her clenched, wet pussy as I moved my cock inside her. On the way she moved beneath me and against me the longer I fucked her.

It felt like an age before her entire body clenched and she went rigid beneath me. Her cry of pleasure filled my room, and it took mere seconds for me to join her in an orgasm. My balls throbbed and my cock pulsed as I came, lowering my mouth to take hers in a firm kiss that drowned out my groan.

Our bodies were slick with sweat, and it took everything inside me not to collapse on top of her. Her short, harsh breaths were hot against my skin, and she slowly relaxed her grip on me until the sting from her nails dissipated.

She ran her hands over my back. Her fingers were so soft compared to her nails, and I relaxed under her confident touch.

"Burgers and an orgasm," Lauren breathed, rolling her head to the side. "This fake relationship might work like a real one after all."

"Homemade burgers," I reminded her, sitting up straight to ease my cock out of her. Her hips bucked as I pulled out of her and released her legs. "Homemade makes a big difference."

"It does." She blew out a long breath and after sitting up herself, ran her fingers through my hair. "I'm stealing your conditioner."

"My what?" I got up and rolled off the condom.

"Your conditioner. Your hair is soft. I'm jealous."

"I don't know what that is."

"You don't know what conditioner is?"

"I use the same thing for my body and my hair."

Lauren flopped down onto her back again dramatically. "Men. You get it so easy."

"Get an erection in a pair of jeans and then tell me we have it easy."

"Your horniness goes down. My horniness stays in a damp patch in my panties."

"I'm so glad we had sex before you said that."

"Same. But, just so you know, there are more genius little quips where that came from." She groaned as she rolled over and got up. "Where's the bathroom? Do you have anything I can use as a… you know."

I peered back at her over my shoulder. "I don't know."

"A wedge. For drippage purposes."

Slowly, I turned around, meeting her eyes as I did so. "For what purposes?"

"Drippage. You'd put a cup under a leaking radiator, wouldn't you?"

"Yes. Are you saying you need a cup for your vagina when we're done having sex?"

She cocked a brow. "No. I don't want to catch the excess to water my plants, Mason. A towel will do just fine."

I had no response to that except for laughter. I'd literally pay anyone who could come up with something to say to that.

"Would you like a towel?" was what I finally settled on.

"I'd love a towel. Thanks."

I grabbed one from the radiator and threw it across the room to her. "I'll make a note to keep one within reach on your side of the bed."

"My side of the bed? Ooh, you fancy." She stood and stuffed the towel between her legs. She was stark naked otherwise, and it was quite the fucking sight. "You want a picture?"

"Of you with a towel between your legs? No. Of my cock between them? It's a little too early for that, isn't it?"

She waddled across the room, holding the towel in place with one hand and her tits with the other. "Holy shit, we're gonna have to find a middle ground on the witty, snarky chat here. You're exhausting."

"Given that you just came so hard you need a towel between your legs, I'll take 'exhausting' as a compliment."

Lauren shot me a look as she continued her penguin-like walk into the bathroom. She shut the door behind her, leaving me standing where I was, shaking my head.

Then, out of nowhere, I laughed.

I'd just watched the woman I was falling for waddle into the bathroom with a towel between her legs, and here I was, laughing.

Yet it all made sense.

That was why I was laughing.

She was fucking funny. She was shameless. She didn't care what anyone thought of her unless she cared about them, too—but right now, she really didn't care.

She was so goddamn real it hurt.

Had I ever seen another woman shove a towel between

their legs in case of 'drippage?'

No.

Never in my life.

But Lauren—fuck me. I'd said it a thousand times, and I had a feeling I'd say it a thousand more: she was something else.

She was fucking special.

Special.

The bathroom door opened and Lauren stepped out, now wrapped in a different towel entirely.

She paused in front of me. "I put the other towel in your laundry basket. I'll even do your laundry to make up for getting lady juice all over that one."

I sighed. Heavily. "Are you going to be like this in twenty years?"

"No. In twenty years I'll probably be a jaded mother of pre-teens who doesn't have time for sex with you. Enjoy this while you can. I'll be snarking about the lack of bread and milk one day."

"And you'll look just as sexy as you do right now."

"Careful. I might kill you and feed you to the pigs before that happens."

"The pigs? What pigs? Who is getting pigs?"

"We are." She patted my cheek again. "Keep up, soldier. This is your life now."

I tried not to smile, but fuck it, I couldn't.

Yeah, this was early days, but if I knew one thing about Lauren Green, it was this:

She could be the one.

With her snark and her jokes and her shamelessness, she had everything I never knew I wanted in a woman.

And if I had to keep a towel beside my bed and fixings for a burger in my fridge to keep her happy, that's what I would do.

Even if her contribution was the weekly babysitting of a tiny human being whose head was smaller than my hand and cat who liked to sit on my head while I held said baby.

It hadn't happened yet, but I was preparing myself.

I'd take it.

I'd take her laughs and jokes and smiles until my cheeks hurt from doing all that myself. I'd take her craziness and her wildness and her sometimes reservedness, because I knew that beneath it all, Lauren was nothing but a mess of softness and emotion.

And it was that softness that had her wink at me before she delved into my drawers and pulled out one of my old, blue t-shirts. She pulled it over her head, and it absolutely drowned her. It was huge compared to her, falling to her knees and swamping her gorgeous frame.

She sat on the edge of the bed in nothing but that faded, navy t-shirt. Then, she looked at me with her eyes sparkling and said, "I'm hungry. Can I raid your kitchen?"

And that was that.

EPILOGUE

Lauren

Nine Months Later

"HAWAII."

"No. Bali."

"Bali? Do you know how expensive Bali is?"

"Do you know how expensive Hawaii is?"

"Why don't we go somewhere closer? Like Cuba. Or the Bahamas?"

"How about a staycation?" I suggested. "It's too cold to go anywhere now, but we can head somewhere in the summer. Florida is too hot then."

Mason sighed and dropped his head back. "A staycation wasn't how I pictured our first vacation together."

"Yeah, well, Uncle Charlie accidentally sent me nudes last weekend, and I wasn't expecting that, so…"

"Fine, fine, fine. Where are you thinking?"

"I have a couple ideas. We could go to the beach."

"Lauren, babe, we live in Florida. The beach isn't a vacation."

"Ugh. You know what I mean. *This* isn't a vacation." I waved my arm around.

All right, so we were sitting on the beach, but who cared?

"All right. Humor me. Where do you wanna go?"

"There's this little town I know in South Carolina. I went to school with a girl who lives there—her name is Halley. Their town makes a big deal out of summer, and they have this huge festival. She runs the kissing booth and is their reigning champion. It's just inland enough from the beach that's it's not a full beach vacation, but close enough that it is."

Mason leaned across the table. "That's not a vacation. That's a trip."

"Okay, so let's take a trip, then do the vacation to make sure we don't kill each other."

He rubbed his hands down his face. "You know what? That seems like a good idea. Let's do that."

I grinned. "I love it when you agree with me. It's like Christmas all over again."

"Hmm. You're lucky I love you."

"It's not luck at all. You love my charm. It's so endearing."

"I'm surprised you can get anywhere with that ego of yours."

"Well, you carry most of it for me with your sweet words, so…"

Mason smiled playfully, reaching across the table to brush his thumb over my jaw. "I'll make sure to keep those contained in the future."

"Aw. But I like those."

"No. You're taking them to heart too much."

"I also took Pru shopping last week and I'm still scarred from zipping her up. You literally owe me."

"I didn't make you do that. Blame my mother."

"I love your mom."

"I know. You have a little girlmance going on. Whatever. Can we discuss something else now?"

"Like your birthday?"

He reached over and put his finger on my lips. "No. We aren't discussing my birthday."

"Aw." I pouted. "But Henry wants to start planning."

Mason shook his head. "Henry is on my shit list. Because he shit in my shoes."

"He shit in your shoes because you didn't bring him tuna. You know the rules. You started bringing tuna, so now you have to continue."

"Yeah, but how do you explain Cara drooling all over my keys?"

"She's, like, ten months old. You leave your keys where she can get them, and she's going to eat them. That's really all on you."

He sighed and leaned back. "I knew this would be hard work. My shoes are shit in, my keys are covered in baby drool, and my vacation is to South Carolina instead of Hawaii. I don't know why I'm surprised."

I changed seats so I was sitting next to him instead of opposite him and scooted in next to him. "You're not."

He eyed me. "You're right. I'm not."

I grinned, nudging him with my elbow. "Love you."

Mason tried to fight his smile, but he didn't really stand a chance at all. He never did.

It was one of my favorite things about him.

"Yeah, yeah. You're a pain in my ass."

"I know. It's why you love me."

He pressed his lips against the side of my head. "Sure is."

KISS ME NOT

COMING AUGUST 27th!

What do you do when you're the reigning kissing booth champion but the only person you *want* to kiss is your best friend's brother?

Let me make this clear right here, right now: I, Halley Dawson, do not care that Preston Wright is kissing other women.

Not a lick. Not at all. Nuh-uh-*freakin'-uh*.

I do care that he's doing it six feet away from me behind a gaudy velvet curtain—making him my competition in this year's kissing contest.

Why do I care, you ask? Because I've had an unfortunate crush on the insufferable idiot since I was sixteen years old, but I also know it's never going to happen.

He's the Creek Falls bachelor to die for, and I'm the Creek Falls raccoon lady who puts peanut butter sandwiches out for them every night.

I'm not going to let him break my four-year-long reign—no matter how many times he breaks the rules and slides the curtain across to do the one thing he's not allowed to:

Kiss me.

Visit
www.emmahart.net/kiss-me-not
to preorder!

ABOUT THE AUTHOR

Emma Hart is the *New York Times* and *USA TODAY* bestselling author of over thirty novels and has been translated into several different languages.

She is a mother, wife, lover of wine, Pink Goddess, and valiant rescuer of wild baby hedgehogs.

Emma prides herself on her realistic, snarky smut, with comebacks that would make a PMS-ing teenage girl proud.

Yes, really. She's that sarcastic.

You can find her online at:
www.emmahart.org
www.facebook.com/emmahartbooks
www.instagram.com/EmmaHartAuthor
www.pinterest.com/authoremmahart

Alternatively, you can join her reader group at **http://bit.ly/EmmaHartsHartbreakers**.

You can also get all things Emma to your email inbox by signing up for Emma Alerts*. **http://bit.ly/EmmaAlerts**

*Emails sent for sales, new releases, pre-order availability, and cover reveals. Each cover reveal contains an exclusive excerpt.

BOOKS BY EMMA HART

Standalones:

Blind Date
Being Brooke
Catching Carly
Casanova
Mixed Up
Miss Fix-It
Miss Mechanic
The Upside to Being Single
The Hook-Up Experiment
The Dating Experiment
Four Day Fling
Best Served Cold
Tequila, Tequila
Catastrophe Queen
The Roommate Agreement
The Accidental Girlfriend
The Vegas Nights series:
Sin
Lust

Stripped series:

Stripped Bare
Stripped Down

The Burke Brothers:

Dirty Secret
Dirty Past
Dirty Lies
Dirty Tricks

Dirty Little Rendezvous

The Holly Woods Files Mysteries:
Twisted Bond
Tangled Bond
Tethered Bond
Tied Bond
Twirled Bond
Burning Bond
Twined Bond
The Holly Woods Files Mysteries Boxset, 1-4
Tricky Bond (A Short Story)

By His Game series:
Blindsided
Sidelined
Intercepted

Call series:
Late Call
Final Call
His Call

Wild series:
Wild Attraction
Wild Temptation
Wild Addiction
Wild: The Complete Series

The Game series:

The *Love Game*
Playing for Keeps
The Right Moves
Worth the Risk
Memories series:
Never Forget
Always Remember

Printed in Great Britain
by Amazon